TO FALL FOR A KISS

KISS THE WALLFLOWER, BOOK 4

TAMARA
Gill

COPYRIGHT

To Fall For a Kiss
Kiss the Wallflower, Book 4
Copyright © 2019 by Tamara Gill
Cover Art by Wicked Smart Designs
Editor Grace Bradley Editing
Proofread Monique Daoust
All rights reserved.

ISBN 13: 978-0-6487160-2-0

DEDICATION

For my friend, critique partner and fellow author,
Jo Duncan.
I will miss our emails and your unwavering support. Until we meet
again my friend.

PROLOGUE

Covent Garden, London Season, 1809

$\mathcal{L}$ady Clara Quinton, only daughter to the Duke of Law, gingerly backed up against an old elm tree, the laughter and sounds of gaiety beyond the garden hedge mocking her for the silly mistake she'd made. The tree bark bit into her gown and she cringed when Lord Peel would not give her space to move away.

Walking off with Viscount Peel had not been her most intelligent notion after he insisted she see a folly he was fond of. After her acquiescence, her evening had deteriorated further. If she happened to get herself out of this situation it would be the last time she'd come to Covent Garden and certainly the last time she had anything to do with his lordship.

"Please move away, my lord. You're too close."

He threw her a mocking glance, his teeth bright white under the moonlit night. His mouth reeked of spirits and she turned away, looking for anyone who may rescue her. What did he think he was going to do to her? Or get away with, the stupid man? "My lord, I must insist. My father is expecting me back at our carriage."

"Come now, Clara, we've been playing this pretty dance for years. Surely it's time for you to bestow me a kiss. I will not tell a soul. I promise."

She glanced at him. Lord Peel was a handsome man, all charm, tall, and with an abundance of friends and wealth and yet, the dance he spoke of mainly consisted of her trying to get away from him. There was something about the gentleman that made her skin crawl as if worms were slithering over her.

He'd taken an immediate like to her on the night of her debut several years ago, and she'd not been able to remove him from her side since, no matter how much she tried to show little favor to any of the men who paid her court. She was six and twenty and sole heir to her father's many estates. She wanted for nothing, and with so many other things occupying her mind of late, a husband did not fit in with her plans at present.

If she were to marry she would have to leave her father, and she could not do that. Not now when he was so very ill and in all honesty, there had been no one who had sparked her interest, not since Marquess Graham during her coming out year before he up and married a servant. Clara would be lying if she had not felt slighted and confused by his choice.

"If you should try and kiss me, my lord, I shall tell my father of your conduct. I can promise you that. Now move." She pushed at his shoulders and she may as well have been pushing against a log of wood. He didn't budge, simply leaned in closer, clasping her chin and squashing her farther into the tree trunk. She cringed at the pain he induced.

"Do not make me force you, Clara." His voice dropped to a deep whisper full of menace.

Fear rippled through her and she shivered, glancing

beyond his shoulder. Should she scream? To do so would court scandal. People would come scrambling to her aid, and she would be left having to explain why she was alone with Lord Peel in the first place. Especially if they did not have an understanding. Clara could not put her father through such gossip. He had enough on his shoulders without her worrying him with her own mistakes.

"You're a brute. How dare you treat me like this?" She tried to move away once again and as quick as a flash he grabbed her, wresting her to the ground. She did scream then, but with his chest over her face her cry for help was muffled.

Clara pushed at him as he tried to kiss her, his hands hard and rough against her face. "Stop," she said, "please stop."

He merely laughed, the sound mocking, and then in an instant he was gone. For a moment she remained on the ground, trying to figure out what had happened and then she saw him. Mr. Grant, or Stephen Grant, the Marquess Graham's brother-in-law and a man she'd promised to loathe forever and a day. He stood over Lord Peel, his face a mixture of horror and fury. Somewhere in the commotion Mr. Grant must have punched Lord Peel, for he was holding his jaw and there was a small amount of blood on his lip.

Clara scrambled to her feet, wiping at her gown and removing the grass and garden debris from her dress as best she could. Mr. Grant came to her, clasping her shoulders and giving her a little shake. "Are you injured? Did he hurt you at all?"

Clara glanced at Lord Peel as he gained his feet. He glared at Mr. Grant as he too wiped garden debris from his clothing and righted his superfine coat.

"You may leave, Mr. Grant. You're not welcome to intrude in a private conversation I'm having with Lady Clara."

"Private? Mauling someone on the ground is not what I'd consider a conversation, my lord. I heard her shout for assistance. I hardly think the conversation was one of Lady Clara's liking."

Clara moved over toward Mr. Grant when Lord Peel took a menacing step in her direction. An odd thing for her to do as she had never been friends with the man and to seek his protection now went against everything within her. But if she were to remain at Lord Peel's mercy, she would choose Mr. Grant of course. He had two sisters after all, and from what she'd seen over the years he loved them dearly. He would not allow any harm to come to her. Mr. Grant reached out a hand and shuffled her behind him, backing her toward where her father would be waiting with the carriage.

Lord Peel's eyes blazed with anger. "Of course it was to her liking. We're courting, you fool."

She gasped, stepping forward, but Mr. Grant clasped her about the waist and held her back. "How dare you, my lord?" she stated even as Mr. Grant restrained her. "I never once asked for you to pursue me and I never gave you any indication that I wanted you to."

Lord Peel glared at her. Mr. Grant turned her back toward the opening in the hedge where they had entered the small, private space and pushed her on. "Go, Lady Clara. I shall speak to his lordship. I can watch from here to ensure you reach your carriage, which if I'm not mistaken your father is waiting beside and looking for you."

Clara clasped Mr. Grant's hands, squeezing them. "I cannot thank you enough. You have proven to be the best kind of man for coming to the aid of a woman you may not be inclined to help under normal circumstances. I thank you for it."

He threw her a puzzled glance. "Should anyone bellow for help and I hear it, of course I will come. Now go, Lady

Clara. The time apart from your guests has been long enough."

Clara nodded, turning and walking away. She reached up and fixed her hair, hoping it did not look as out of place as it felt. As she walked back toward the revelers, a little of her fear slipped away knowing Mr. Grant watched her. She glanced over her shoulder, and true to his word, Mr. Grant continued to survey her progress and ensure she arrived back at her carriage safely.

A shiver of awareness slid over her skin, completely opposite to what she experienced each time she was in the presence of Lord Peel. She'd always disliked Mr. Grant and his siblings, one of whom married Marquess Graham, her own suitor during her first Season and the man she thought she would marry. He did not offer for her hand, choosing to marry a lady's companion instead.

"There you are, my dear. I've been looking for you."

She reached up and kissed her father's cheek, her legs of a sudden feeling as if they would not hold her for too much longer. "Shall we go, Papa?" she said, taking his arm and guiding him toward the carriage. The coachman bowed before opening the door for them.

"Yes, let us go, my dear. I've had quite enough time in the gardens and watching the *ton* at play."

Clara stepped up into the carriage and sank down on the padded velvet seats, relief pouring through her that no one other than Mr. Grant had come upon her and his lordship in the garden, or the position that they'd been found.

Heat rushed over her cheeks and she picked up the folded blanket on her seat and settled it about her father's legs as the carriage lurched forward. Anything to distract her from the memory of it.

"Shall we ring for tea and play a game of chess when we

arrive home, Papa? It may be a nice way to end the evening just us two together."

Her father glanced at her, a little blank and unsure. "I think I shall retire, my dear. It's been a tiring evening."

"Very well," she said, swallowing the lump in her throat that wedged there each and every time she was around her parent. She knew the reason he no longer liked to play chess, cards or even the piano, at which he'd once been proficient, was because he'd forgotten how. His mind over the last two years had slowly disremembered many things, even some of the servants who had been with them since she was a girl.

Unbeknownst to her father Clara had sought out an opinion with their family doctor and he'd agreed that her father had become more forgetful and vague, and that it may be a permanent affliction.

She sighed. The fact that there was little she could do to help him regain his memory saddened her and as much as she tried to remind him of things, an awful realization that one day he'd forget her had lodged in her brain and would not dissipate.

What would happen after that? Would he still be as healthy as he was now, but with no memory, or would whatever this disease that ailed his mind affect his body as well.

The idea was not to be borne. He was all she had left.

"Maybe tomorrow, Papa, after breakfast perhaps."

He smiled at her, and she grinned back. "Maybe, my dear, or you could ask your mother. I know how very fond of chess she is."

Clara nodded, blinking and looking out the carriage window so he would not see her upset. If only she could ask her mama, who'd been dead these past ten years.

*S*tephen stood between Lord Peel and the man's exit at his back in the gardens. The moment he'd strode into the small, private area and seen a flash of pink muslin and a gentleman forcing a woman into kissing him a veil of red had descended over his eyes and he'd not known how he'd stopped himself from pummeling the man into pulp.

"You will leave Lady Clara alone or I shall speak to her father of what I witnessed this evening. Do you understand, my lord?"

Peel chuckled, the sound mocking and full of an arrogance that Stephen was well aware of with this gentleman. He was also aware that he'd once been married and that his wife had fallen ill not long after their marriage. Of course, upon the young woman's death, Peel had played the widower very well, and had enjoyed the copious amount of money that his young wife had left him, or so Marquess Graham had told him one evening when Stephen had noticed his marked attention toward Lady Clara. A woman who seemed to show little interest in the gentleman trying to court her.

Lord Peel tapped a finger against his chin. "I forget... Do I need to listen to you? What is your name... Mr. Grant, isn't it? Son of nobody."

Stephen fisted his hands at his sides, reminding himself that to break the fellow's nose would not do him or his sisters any good now that they were part of the sphere this mongrel resided within. He'd already hit him once, to bloody him up too much would not do.

"You are correct. I'm Mr. Stephen Grant of Nobody of Great Import, but I will say this... You're no one of import either if the rumors about you and your conduct are to be believed."

Lord Peel's face mottled red and Stephen was glad his words struck a chord in the bastard. He needed to hear some truths and to know that his marked attention toward women, his inability to grasp that he saw them as nothing but playthings for his enjoyment had been noted and talked about. He pushed past Stephen and he let him go, not wanting to waste another moment of his time on such a nob.

The gentleman's retreating footsteps halted. "Lady Clara will be my wife. I will be speaking to her father soon about my proposal and I will have her. I am a viscount. It is only right that Lady Clara marry a man such as myself, so if you look to her as a possible candidate as your wife, you'll be sadly mistaken. Move on and marry a tavern wench, that'll suit your status better. A duke's daughter is not for you."

Stephen glared at the man's back as he disappeared into the throng of revelers still dancing and enjoying their night in Covent Garden. "Yes, well, Lord Peel, she's not for you either and I'll be damned if I'll let you have her."

CHAPTER 1

Autumn – 1809

Clara settled the blanket about her father's legs and sat on a settee beside the fire. They had returned to Chidding Hall a fortnight past, and autumn this year had been windy and wet, a sure sign that winter would be cold. The fire crackled and popped, and with the velvet drapes pulled closed, the candles burning in the library, the room was warm and inviting, a perfect place to relax and enjoy some time together.

Something that had been happening less and less. Her father, since the end of the season, had deteriorated so severely that she'd ended her time in London early and had returned home to Kent without delay.

He'd improved since being away from town, and the many outings she feared took a toll on him and made him more vulnerable to bouts of anxiety, clumsiness and confusion. Home at least, her father was more relaxed and he'd been better, but still, something inside Clara told her that his illness would only get worse. It was certainly the trajectory he'd been on at least.

"Did I tell you that I received word today that we have a new neighbor? Moved in last week."

Clara placed the letter from her friend in London down in her lap. "Really? What estate? I've not heard of any estate being up for sale or lease." She knew all the particulars regarding their neighbors in the county. Having worked with the steward for the past three years, there was little she didn't know now about her tenants, the land and surrounding neighbors.

Her father's eyes twinkled, no doubt pleased that he knew something she did not. "Oh yes, a Mr. Grant has leased Ashby Cottage, his brother-in-law's home. It's been empty for so many years. I've not seen anyone living there since Lord Graham's grandmother resided there. It'll be good to have someone in it again. I always believe that when a house sits empty it deteriorates. Lord Graham has maintained the upkeep on the estate however, so I do not think there will be much needed to be done by Mr. Grant to ensure his comfort."

Clara listened as her father rattled on about the gentleman and she ignored the fluttering that overtook her stomach at the mention of his name. Mr. Grant was their new neighbor? She picked up her letter, feigning reading. "That is good news, both for the estate and the local county. Another home open will mean more employment for the local people." She paused, folding and unfolding the corner of the letter lying in her lap. "I met Mr. Grant several years ago in London, on recent acquaintance his character has improved, I'm happy to say."

Certainly he'd been an ogre the first time they had met in Hyde Park. She'd come across him, his sister and Marquess Graham not long after his lordship's marriage. It may not have been the nicest thing to have done, but to see his lord-ship flaunting his new wife, and her brother growling at anyone who dared mention their less-than-pleasing heritage had brought out the worst side of her. She'd been terribly rude, but then Mr. Grant had also. After that she'd not gone out of her way to mend ties with the family.

"That is very good to hear," her father said, smiling.

"I shall have Cook send a basket of our produce as a welcome." That would do nicely and she'd include a small note stating her own thanks for his assistance in Covent Garden. That should do the trick and end any future need to associate with him.

Her father leaned back in his chair, crossing his legs out before him. "No, you shall deliver it, instead of a servant. We're the highest-ranked family in the county, it is your duty to invite him for dinner and welcome him properly."

Clara gasped, unable to hide her dismay at having to do such a thing. "A basket from our servants will be just as well received as one from me. I do not need to go, Papa, and now that I no longer have a companion I do not see the point in making my maid travel with me, through this cold and damp weather simply to deliver a basket of food. One of the stable hands can deliver it. That will do well enough."

Her father looked at her, his brow furrowed. "Why do you no longer have a companion?"

Clara blinked, fighting back tears at his inability to remember details of their life. "Mrs. Humphries remarried three years ago, Papa. Do you not remember? You gave her away in our church."

He blinked at her several times before his eyes cleared and she knew he remembered. "Oh of course, how forgetful I am. Well then, we'll have to get you a new companion."

"I'm six and twenty, Papa. I do not need one. Most of my friends are married now, if I design to go out with them, they can act as my chaperone." The reminder that she was the last of her friend set to be wed had caused her many nights of unease, but then as sole heiress to her father's estates there was little reason to worry.

After losing Marquess Graham to a servant of all people, the desire to marry had waned. Not because she was still in love with his lordship, for she was not. She'd long ago recognized that her infatuation with him had been a youthful folly, but having seen him with his wife, the devotion and love he showed her and the *ton* was what she wanted for herself.

During the past eight years since her debut, she'd refused to settle for anyone who did not make her heart flutter and her stomach too. Not only that, but she wanted a gentleman who was intelligent, could offer an opinion without worrying what others thought of him. All the gentlemen who had courted her had been less than pleasing.

"Even so, my dear, I think it would be best that you welcome Mr. Grant to our county. Your approval of him will ensure his acceptance from the other families of our set."

Clara sighed, preferring not to see Mr. Grant again, but then, she supposed she ought to thank him properly for coming to her aid during the Season. His intrusion had thankfully kept Lord Peel away from her, at least at the events that Mr. Grant also attended. She'd not been able to talk to him there, however. Shame washed over her at the reason as to why.

Her friends knew of her dislike of him and his sisters and so she felt bound to keep up the pretense of indifference, even though he'd come to her aid. But then he'd not sought her out either, to see if she were well and recovered and so it seemed their association, no matter how short in duration, was at an end.

"Very well, Papa. I shall deliver a basket tomorrow. That

will satisfy my obligations and we shall be done with any further need to show hospitality."

Her father chuckled, leaning his head back and closing his eyes. "You talk as if you fear Mr. Grant, Clara." He opened one eye and inspected her. She fought not to fidget under his regard. "He is just a man, my dear. Nothing to cause distress, I'm sure."

Of course he was right, but still, even now after speaking of him her wretched body refused not to squirm at the mention of his name. It was simply because he'd caught her in a compromising position and was a gentleman whom she disliked. To be indebted to someone you had always loathed was not to be borne and was the reason why she did not feel herself. She was silly to imagine anything else.

Stephen kicked off his boots at the servants' entrance after having walked about the grounds of his new home. His brother-in-law, the Marquess Graham had offered to lease the property, to let him make use of the house and land as he chose. His lordship had been contemplating selling the estate for some time, due to being unused since his grandmother's time, subsequent to her passing.

The house was on a good-sized property with three hundred acres that his lordship had said Stephen could use for income. His brother-in-law had also been lenient and allowed him to lease the property for less than what it was worth and he'd forever be indebted to him. Stephen wasn't fool enough not to know he did any of this for him. The man was devoted to his sister Louise and would do anything to make her and her family happy.

Since the marriage of his sister, Sophie, the Marquess had gone to great pains to ensure Stephen remained close to

Louise and wouldn't, too, hightail it off to Scotland and live there. They had been separated as children and the Marquess did not want that again for his wife.

He walked without shoes into the foyer, his clothing damp and muddy after tracking down to the local waterway that ran through his property. He ran a hand through his wet hair and came to a sliding stop at the sight of Lady Clara staring at him, her mouth agape and her eyes stealing over his person from head to foot.

For a moment he didn't say a word, merely took in her perfectly styled hair, a bonnet dangling from blue ribbons in her gloved hand. Her gown was of a deeper shade of the sky and with her overcoat, she looked warm and inviting. He shivered, aware that he at least looked the complete opposite to her, a wreck, a wet and muddy mess.

She raised her brows, meeting his eyes and his defenses shot up. He'd seen that look before, many times in fact in London over the years when she judged him and his family, looked down at him along that pretty, pert nose of hers.

He stilled at the thought. She wasn't pretty, and what the hell had made him think such a thing? He started for the library, needing to escape her presence and the falsehood he'd just told himself. "Apologies, Lady Clara, but I must get dry. I've been out overlooking the property and have grown damp."

She followed him, her light footsteps close on his heels. "Yes, Papa said Marquess Graham had leased the property to you. How very fortunate you are."

He clamped his jaw shut, making the fire and turning to warm his backside. Heat seeped into his bones, a welcome reprieve from the chilling outdoors. "Mocking me already? I thought that perhaps my coming to your aid in London may have halted the barbed words that so often spewed from your lips toward my person." They had never been wont to hide their dislike of each other, and Stephen had always found when it came to Lady Clara, to speak frankly was always best.

She raised her chin, and his gaze took in her features before dropping to her lips, now puckered into a mulish line. Damn it, he'd always liked her defiance, especially when he said or did something that vexed her.

"What a delightful way of putting it, Mr. Grant. I see living in a gentleman's house, circulating within the upper echelons of the *ton* has not improved your common manners. You will need to do better if you're to fit in with our society here."

He shrugged, bringing attention to the fact his shirt was damp. He reached behind him and pulled it off over his head. Of course to do so was courting scandal and ungentlemanly to the extreme, but the woman was a vexing little prig and he wanted to shock her. If she thought he was so very common, then he'd act like a common man not afraid to undress before a lady. No matter who she was.

"I do not need to fit in with the society here. If they shun me, that is their choice and problem. I'll not change to please others. Unlike some people whom I've seen throughout the years I've been in London." Namely the chit glaring at him right now.

She gasped, dropping the basket he only just noticed she was holding on a nearby table. "I suppose you mean me, Mr. Grant. How dare you be so rude? I demand an apology at once."

"I will not apologize for stating the truth and I did not name names, Lady Clara. You think too highly of yourself if you believe I was talking about your person." Although he very well meant her and her gaggle of silly friends, all of whom had married men whom he'd seen frequent the clubs about London and had seen the indiscretions they partook in. All but Lady Clara had succumbed to the marriage state. He narrowed his eyes upon her.

Why though, he could not make out. She was a duke's daughter, an heiress, a perfect catch for the gentlemen of London and beyond.

It was probably because no one exceeded her lofty aspirations of what constituted a good husband. He walked over to her, ignoring the fact her eyes slid over his now-naked chest like a caress. His skin prickled and he wondered what her hands on his skin would feel like.

Damn good he'd imagine.

He shook the thought aside, opening the basket. "What do you have here? A present for me?"

She rolled her eyes and he bit back a grin. "Father wanted me to welcome you to the neighborhood. He insisted I deliver it. Now that I have, I shall take my leave."

He glanced down at her, noticing her blonde locks were only partly pulled up on her head. The few strands that sat about her shoulders only accentuated her pretty neck. She was not a tall woman, only coming up to his chin, but even so, neither was she short, considering his height.

"You did not wish to deliver them yourself? I thought we may be friends after Covent Garden."

A flash of fear slid into her blue orbs before she blinked and it was gone. Even so, he'd seen it and understood the fear his words had brought forth. Lord Peel's treatment of her that night obviously haunted her, and scared her still.

Stephen sighed, ashamed to have teased her just then. "I apologize, Lady Clara. I should not make light of that situation. Please forgive me." He returned to the fire, keeping his back to her. "I thank you for the basket. I'll be sure to call on your father in the coming days to introduce myself and give my thanks for your generosity."

When she didn't venture to reply, he turned and found

her gaze locked on his lower back. Her eyes widened and she looked at him as if seeing him for the first time. He couldn't help the grin that formed on his lips. He supposed it was only natural. She'd probably not seen many men so scantily dressed in her life.

"Lady Clara? Did you hear what I said?"

She nodded, licking her lips. His body hardened at the sight of her tongue. For all her harshness toward him and his sisters, her lofty airs and disdain for those she did not see fit to wipe her boots, damn it she was beautiful. There was no use trying to deny the truth of that fact, and he was a fool to try to sway his mind that she was not. Lady Clara was a sweet little morsel that was ripe for plucking. Not that he'd be the one to pluck her, but still, he wasn't blind to her outer beauty. What a pity her inner self was so very rotten.

"Of course I heard and my current thoughts are those that I hope you learn to dress yourself better when you arrive. I was also charged to invite you to dine with us tomorrow evening. Maybe your valet can guide you on what is appropriate to wear around a lady. What you have on at present is not."

He ground his teeth, wanting to retort in kind, and yet he did not. His pants were uncomfortably damp and he needed her to leave so he could change. He doubted that Lady Clara would appreciate it if he undid his breeches and pulled those off in front of her as well.

"I shall ensure I pass on your advice to my valet." A servant he'd not deemed necessary and actually did not have. He'd been dressing himself since he was eight, he wasn't now about to need another man to assist him. "Your advice is so very welcome, my lady."

She rolled her eyes and his lips twitched. "I will bid you good day, Mr. Grant. Dinner is at eight sharp. Try not to be late." He watched as she turned and flounced out of the room without a backward glance.

"I shall do my very best to read the time correctly, Lady Clara, so as not to disappoint you," he called out after her.

He chuckled at the vexed *argh* that came from the foyer before the front door closed softly behind her. Stephen walked to the window and watched as she jumped back into the waiting carriage parked in front of the house before it rattled off down the drive.

Dinner with the Duke of Law and his daughter. He shook his head at the thought of it. Who would have thought he'd be doing such a thing? Certainly he had not, but after Louise and now Sophie's exalted marriages he was forced to endure this society simply due to whom he was now related. An earl and a marquess.

Stephen turned and started for his room, ordering hot water from a waiting footman as he passed him in the foyer. He would do the pretty, play the gentleman, and then his duty would be done with Lady Clara and her father. He could tolerate her for one more night and do his utmost to be on his best behavior before the Duke. If not for the little hellcat who was his neighbor, but then for his sisters and the reputation they wished to keep within the society they circulated.

CHAPTER 2

*C*lara sat at the dining table the following evening and fought not to roll her eyes each and every time Mr. Grant opened his mouth and talked to her father, or at least tried to. Her father this evening seemed quite preoccupied with the table decorations and was continually staring and touching them as if he'd never seen embroidered linen before in his life.

It was only the three of them this evening, and she regretted the decision in not making some of their other neighbors attend and make welcome Mr. Grant. With her father ignoring everyone it was left to her to ensure conversation flowed and it was not a task she wished to do. Not with Mr. Grant in any case. He may have saved her at Covent Garden, but it did not make up for the many times he'd been rude to her in town.

A small voice reminded Clara that she'd been rude also, atrociously so, and especially toward his sisters, so it was only logical that she would receive some criticism in return. Even so, his rudeness had been beyond what she thought was necessary.

"Are you enjoying the venison, Mr. Grant? The deer came from our lands, we have hundreds running about." She stared down at the meat on her plate, furiously thinking of what else she could talk about. If they resorted to talking of the weather the evening would be a terrible bore. Perhaps horses? Or even the tablecloth, at least then maybe her papa would take part.

"It is very good…deer."

She looked up and read the laughter glinting in his blue-green eyes, having not missed the double entendre to his words. Was he trying to be amusing? If so, he was not succeeding.

"How are your sisters, Mr. Grant? I heard Miss Sophie has moved to Scotland and is settled."

All amusement fled from his eyes and she marveled at her triumph. Good, at least the subject of his siblings he did not find amusing, especially when it was she who was querying about them. No doubt he'd steeled himself for her to be cutting in regard to his sisters. For years they had played this game of who could insult the other better. It was only natural he would assume she would not stop, even if before her father.

"Both my sisters are doing well. Louise has recently traveled to Scotland to be with Sophie during the birth of her second child. She has returned to London now, however."

"What a shame you did not go," she said, smiling to soften her insinuation that he ought to leave and never come back. "But I suppose moving into Marquess Graham's country estate is more important for a young man on the rise." She smiled sweetly. "I hope Lady Mackintosh came through the birth well."

He stared at her nonplused and she kept her smile firmly on her lips. At least if he'd gone to Scotland she'd not be forced to host dinner parties and think of things to say to please their guest. In future, no matter what her father said, she would agree, but then not follow through on any such ideas. Her father had not taken part in the evening in any case, he may as well have stayed in the library where he was most comfortable for all the conversation he'd taken part in.

"Sophie tolerated the birth well. I will travel up to Moy in the coming months after I finish moving into Ashby Cottage. I wish to lord about the house and grounds for some weeks and think myself very grand and important. I must act, you see, just as my betters do. People such as yourself. I have little doubt that you keep a steely eye on all those working for the estate."

She raised one brow. Had he really said what he just did? Clara took a sip of wine, watching him over the rim of the crystal glass. "I do of course, just as any proficient landlord should. You forget, Mr. Grant, I'm an educated woman in possession of a brain and know how to keep not just one, but multiple estates running well."

"Clara dear, do you think the roses are happy being on our table? They look a little sad to me."

Mr. Grant turned his attention to the roses, reaching out to pick one. "I think, your Grace, that they are the happiest when before those who appreciate beauty, like now, as the centerpiece of your dining table."

Clara did not know what to say to Mr. Grant's kind words to her father. Very few, except for her father's valet, the butler and housekeeper knew that the Duke was falling ill of mind. Mr. Grant being here this evening could soon change that fact. He'd likely tell everyone he knew that the Duke of Law was addled completely.

He'd take pleasure in embarrassing her and her family she was sure, a revenge of sorts after the many years that they had not gotten along.

"You look a little tired, Papa. Do you want me to ring for James?"

Her father's eyes cleared and just like that she knew he was with them again. "Not yet, my dear. The night is still early." He turned to Mr. Grant. "I'm going to go on a fox hunt tomorrow. Have some friends coming up from London for the sport. Would you like to join me?"

Clara inwardly sighed as the fox hunt her father was talking about took place two years ago shortly before his decline.

"That would be wonderful, your Grace. I shall be here before eleven."

The Duke stood, seemingly finished with the conversation and Clara watched as he wandered about the room before walking out the door. She turned to a waiting footman. "Please escort the Duke to his room. James will take over from there."

"Of course, Lady Clara," the servant said, bowing and leaving to do as she bid.

She read the confusion in Mr. Grant's gaze and knew there was little she could do but to explain, as best she could in any case.

"Apologies for my father, Mr. Grant, over the last several months his heath has declined, his memory most of all. I need you to understand that there is no fox hunt tomorrow. The fox hunt he invited friends up from London for took place two years ago around this time, but we have not hosted one since."

He leaned back in his chair, a thoughtful expression on his face. "I'm very sorry to hear this, Lady Clara. You will tell me if there is anything that I can do. I know we're not the best of friends, but all of that is forgotten when one is in need."

She hoped she could believe that with this man. Certainly

in the past he'd had an uncanny ability to speak his mind and to go into battle for those he thought were being mistreated. She'd certainly been on the receiving end of a tongue-lashing from him a time or two.

"Thank you for understanding. The doctor does not seem to know what has brought this ailment on, but he believes it'll be lifelong." Horrifyingly, tears sprung to her eyes at the thought of her father succumbing to his illness and she blinked furiously, lest the one man she was loath to see her upset saw her rattled.

"Truly, my lady. I'm sorry that this has happened to the Duke and yourself. I should not have come here tonight."

She waved his concerns aside, knowing there would be many more days like this one where her father would be vague before guests and tongues would start to wag. "Father invited you, and no matter that sometimes he does not seem to know where he is or what he's doing, having a little normalcy to his life is all I can do for him. If a friend visits, or he invites a new neighbor to dine with us, I will not stop him. In those moments when he is his old self, and I have not done what he's asked, I would never hear the end of his displeasure, so it's easier to be complicit."

Mr. Grant chuckled, the sound deep and warm. Clara studied his strong jaw, straight nose and features that were similar to those of his sisters'. He had a pleasing face for a man who was not nobility and did not come from such exalted stock. Her attention snapped to his attire, his wide, broad shoulders and arms that bulged a little under his superfine coat when he cut into his meal. For all that they were enemies, Clara could admit that as a woman looking at a man, he was far superior to the many men she knew. Pity he was so very far beneath her notice and social status.

*S*tephen cut into his venison and tried to eat his meal as quickly as he could. Seated across from Lady Clara, he had the odd sensation that she was sizing him up and finding fault. He chanced a look at her and yes, sure as the sun rose in the east, she was inspecting him. He inwardly swore. *Please do not think of me romantically.* He wasn't interested.

When he married... No, *if* he married, he'd marry a woman who knew a day's hard work, a woman who was capable, intelligent and empathetic to those less fortunate. A woman who knew how to survive without servants at her every beck and call. Not like the duke's daughter across from him. He doubted Lady Clara knew what a broom was. Not that he would expect his wife to do such menial chores—they would have servants for such matters—but he wanted to know that she at least was capable. He certainly was.

He picked up his glass of wine, taking a sip. He would not let what Lady Clara told him about her father sway his idea of the woman. Her tongue was still as sharp as a blade, and the insults they'd passed between them were too many to count. Far too many to forgive.

He would, however, help her should she need it in regard to her father. To see a man well respected and liked within the society be brought low by illness was never a pleasant thing.

"If I should be fortunate enough to meet your father again, I will not make a scene should he become fuddled or confused, you have my word. Now that I know he's suffering from such an illness, I shall do my very best should I see him to keep him out of harm's away."

"Thank you, Mr. Grant. That is a comfort to me."

Stephen pushed his plate away. A footman offered dessert and he declined. It was time he returned home and he was sure Lady Clara wished to check in on her father in any case. "Please thank your father for the invitation to dinner, but I think I should return home. It's been a pleasure, Lady Clara."

She watched him from across the table, a small smile playing about her lips. "A little advice, Mr. Grant. Such words are normally spoken when one is taking their leave, near the front door or in the parlor after dinner. Not at the dining table."

And there she was again, the little *so and so* who couldn't help but criticize him or his conduct. He stood, walking to the door and leaving her gaping after him. "Goodnight, Lady Clara," he said at the threshold. "I do hope this door is adequate enough for me to take my leave, or do you want to escort me into the hall to satisfy your rules?"

He heard her annoyed sigh and left. The woman bothered him terribly. There was something about her that niggled under his skin like a maggot in cheese.

"Perfectly adequate, thank you," she called after him, taking the last word.

Stephen took his greatcoat from a waiting footman, the cool, fresh country air minimizing his annoyance at Lady Clara just a little. He waited while his horse was brought around and looked out over the ducal lands. The gardens were manicured, not a blade of grass dared be out of place, and even from where he stood, and the encroaching dark, he could tell the property would be even more magnificent during daylight hours.

Maybe if he were invited here again he would get a chance to see its glory. It was certainly the only thing he wished to see at the estate. Certainly the daughter was not a priority in future travels.

CHAPTER 3

Several days later, Clara sat under ferns at the base of the garden. She squinted, focusing on a large hare that sat in the grass looking about for any threats. Clara adjusted her rifle that sat atop a fallen tree log in her hand, trying to get a better position.

The housekeeper had asked her about tonight's dinner and her father had requested rabbit. She'd not seen one of those yet today, but a hare would do well enough and her father would not know the difference.

It sat still, not moving from its own cover and Clara wondered if it would ever walk out into the open so she may have a clean shot.

A bird flew out of the brush and the hare darted away and out of sight. She cursed the little devil and stood, knowing she would have little chance of catching him now that he'd been spooked.

"Maybe tomorrow, Lady Clara," the gamekeeper said, a rifle over his arm and a small smile playing about his mouth. Mr. Wilson had been with the family for as long as Clara could remember. Her father was especially fond of him and his knowledge of animals and wildlife was beyond comprehension.

"Perhaps, but today will not be the day. Father is quite adamant he has rabbit, so do you think you could try and shoot one if you have time?"

He tipped his hat, reaching out a hand to take her gun as she gained her feet. "Of course, my lady. I will ensure the dining table has rabbit on it this evening for his Grace."

"Thank you." She turned toward the house when the sound of voices carried over to her. She stumbled at seeing Mr. Grant walking toward her with her father. He was looking at her curiously, and she could hazard a guess as to why. She supposed he'd not thought her capable of catching her own food. Which, in truth, she had not done today, but on many other days she'd had more success. Clara leaned up and kissed her father's cheek. "Papa. Mr. Grant. How lovely to see you again so soon."

Mr. Grant looked over to where their gamekeeper stood. Clara turned and watched as Mr. Wilson adjusted the guns and then walked into the trees.

"Lady Clara, I did not know you knew how to hunt."

She took her father's arm, leading him back toward the house. "There are a great many things I should imagine you do not know about me, Mr. Grant."

"She's an excellent shot," her father added to the conversation. Clara smiled, a burst of happiness filling her that her father should remember such a detail. There were times when she wondered if he recognized her, never mind what she was capable of.

"I'm not so very good at using a gun. I was not part of any shooting or fox hunting parties when growing up."

The reminder that Mr. Grant had been poor as a child eliminated the barb that she was about to say about a gentleman's worth when one could not shoot. Similar to those little insults often heaped onto a woman's shoulders. That being if they could not sew, draw or play the piano. Instead, Clara found herself saying, "Having your own estate now, Mr. Grant, we shall have to remedy that lapse."

Her father patted her hand with vigor. "Of course. Of course you shall. That is the best idea, my dear. And as you're so proficient in it, you shall be the one to teach Mr. Grant."

Mr. Grant mumbled reasons as to why that would not suit at the same time that Clara pointed out the facts as to why she could not teach him. She would need a chaperone and the gamekeeper was already too busy and so too was her maid to go trudging around the estate teaching a man how to shoot a gun.

"Nonsense," her father said, quelling both their words. "You're more than capable, Clara, and now that we're home you have time on your side. A day or two each week is not too much to ask for our new neighbor."

Clara fought not to show the dismay that coursed through her at the idea of teaching Mr. Grant anything. They were not friends, having never got along well in the past, and should her father be of his right mind, he would never allow her to escort an unmarried gentleman about the grounds for a shooting lesson. The idea was atrocious.

Not to mention that they could have a disagreement and she'd be tempted to shoot him in the foot!

"If you wish, Papa. Of course I'll help Mr. Grant learn the ways of a gentleman."

Mr. Grant met her eyes and she saw the challenge in them. She also recognized that he was dearly fighting to hold back some caustic remark that would annoy her.

She smiled. "Shall we return to the house for tea?" she asked, all sweetness.

Her father nodded, pulling her forward. "That sounds just the thing."

mm, yes, just the thing. Stephen caught up to the Duke and Lady Clara, his hands itching not to strangle the little minx who at any opportunity afforded to her, bothered him. He no more wanted to learn how to shoot with her than she wanted to teach him. He was only here to see the Duke and ask if it would be all right for him to fish in the river that ran adjacent to his property and was owned by his Grace.

Another neighbor had said that there was good perch to be caught in the Duke's stream, but it was unlikely he'd allow him to fish there, stating his Grace was quite protective of his own fish and game. Not that he'd had any trouble in gaining approval, the Duke only seemed too happy to allow him to fish there after he'd asked.

"Oh, and by the by, my dear, I've given Mr. Grant the right to fish in our stream. You know the place, up near farmer Coe's cottage, on the bend where it is deepest."

She glanced at him in surprise. Obviously she was quite aware that her father did not give approval for such occupations often. "As long as Mr. Grant does not fish it out."

Stephen fought not to roll his eyes at the ridiculousness of the comment. "I'm sure I can control myself, Lady Clara. There will be plenty of fish left for you." And bullheaded came to mind when he thought of her.

She raised her chin, not deigning to reply. They strode for a time in quiet, just the sounds of the birds and the gardeners who worked in the beds could be heard. Stephen thought over the Duke, and his mannerisms and words the last two days. There was certainly something not quite right, and after Lady Clara's warning yesterday, he'd seen flashes of the Duke's mind coming and going. Even in the last half hour that he'd been here the Duke had been vague one minute and sharp the next. How much longer would Lady Clara be able to look after him by herself? And would the disease, whatever it was, become worse to the point that the Duke did not know or recognize anyone about him? Even his daughter?

A terrible thought, but one could not help but have it after observing him.

"Mr. Grant will not fish us out, my dear. I see no harm in it. Many people fish there and we've never had any issues yet with stock numbers."

Lady Clara rubbed her father's arm, a confused frown between her brows. "Papa, you never allow anyone to fish there, remember? Mr. Grant is the first you've ever approved."

His Grace stared at Lady Clara and Stephen could read the confusion, the blankness behind the eyes. The poor soul had no idea he'd given him the first approval ever.

"No, you must be mistaken, Clara. I cannot see myself being so difficult to my neighbors who requested such leave."

"Perhaps I'm mistaken, Papa," she conceded, obviously not willing to press the point. "Let us go indoors before it rains. I think there is weather coming in."

They walked up to the terrace and Stephen went ahead, opening the terrace door for the Duke. Clara stopped at the threshold, staring up at him. Her defiant chin rose, and her wide, blue eyes stared down her pert nose at him. How she managed it since she was shorter than he was, was beyond him. But she did and he found himself drawn to taking in every nuance, every little freckle that flittered across her nose and cheeks. He'd thought her skin had been perfectly unblemished, but it was not and it only made her more approachable, more real. He ground his teeth. He would not see her as an attractive woman. He'd be betraying himself should he stoop to such a level.

"You need not stay, Mr. Grant. You have your approval from Papa, no need to have tea."

He feigned injury, clasping his chest in mock pain all the while holding the door open. "You wound me, my lady. If I leave now, how will I ever recover from not taking tea with the most sought-after woman in the *ton* at her country estate? My reputation will never recover."

"Are you two coming in or are you going to have a tête-à-tête in the doorway for the remainder of the day?"

The Duke's words pulled him from thoughts of how fun it was to annoy the chit who stared up at him with loathing. He knew why she hated him so much—he'd been poor, and his sister had married her future betrothed. In her mind in any case.

The thought of her being married soured his temper and he stalked indoors, leaving her standing in the doorway alone.

She gasped and he ignored her shock. Stephen bowed before the Duke. "I thank you for the invitation for tea, your Grace, but I must be off. I hired a man of business and have to meet him this afternoon to discuss the estate and lands."

"Do not let us keep you, Mr. Grant." Lady Clara flopped down on a nearby settee, reaching for the teapot that a servant had brought in without having to be told. How delightful it must be to have people waiting on them hand and foot. He'd become accustomed to a similar lifestyle, but it never sat well with him. To this day he felt as though he were impersonating someone else, should be the one serving the lords and ladies instead of taking tea with them.

Lady Clara thought this way about him still and it irked. More than irked, it irritated the hell out of him. She was an uppity little snob.

"Are you sure, Mr. Grant? You're more than welcome."

His attention flicked to Lady Clara at the Duke's declaration and her little gag of repulsion was not hard to decipher. He shook his head. "Alas, no, but I will call again soon. You're more than welcome to come fishing with me, your Grace. It may be nice to get outdoors and away from meddling females."

The Duke glanced at his daughter and then burst into laughter. Stephen smiled, pleased to have made the Duke laugh and annoyed his daughter at the same time before his leaving.

"Father may attend any event he wishes, I shall not stop him." She picked up her tea and took a sip. "He shall be able to count how many you catch, ensure that you're not taking more than you're welcome to."

The Duke laughed harder and Stephen narrowed his eyes. He took a calming breath, bowing to Lady Clara also. "Good day to you both. I'll see myself out."

Lady Clara's smirk was enough to make him swear, or kiss her smart little mouth quiet. He strode to the door, thanking a footman who handed him his coat from when he arrived. A servant went to fetch his horse, and he kicked his heels in the foyer for a minute as his mount was brought around.

However would he survive living so close to such a woman? He would write to his brother-in-law in London and ask if he had any other estates that he'd like leased in other counties. Maybe he could move to Scotland and live in a cottage on Sophie and Brice's land. To live here, to have to put up with Lady Clara was too much, and yet on his ride home all he could see in his mind's eye was her pretty little nose up in the air as she met his barbs with some of her own and he cursed himself a fool for thinking it charming.

CHAPTER 4

*C*lara stood and walked to the window, watching as Mr. Grant gained his mount and cantered off down the drive. She told herself it was because she wanted to ensure he left her lands, hadn't loitered about and managed to stay longer than he needed to. It wasn't, however, why she was staying where she was in the library, staring after him as his bottom sat snug in his saddle, his back ramrod straight as if he'd been riding his whole life, not only a few years.

He looked very well indeed on the back of a horse. She mumbled words no lady should know and turned back to her father. "It's started to rain. I think Mr. Grant will be soaked through by the time he arrives home."

Her father glanced up at her, a biscuit with jam on top partway to his mouth. "Mr. Grant was here? Why did he not come and see me? I like that fellow, good chap. We should invite him 'round for dinner one evening."

Clara nodded, biting back the sting of tears at her father's words. She looked back out the window and the rain that was falling much heavier, torrential even. A flash of light blazed outside the window followed by a boom of thunder that made her jump.

The thought of Mr. Grant out in this weather was not a pleasant thought, no matter how much they did not get along, how much they disliked each other's company. Mr. Grant out in this storm was dangerous. He could be hit by lightning or his horse could bolt with fright and leave him injured, or worse, dead in a ditch.

"Mr. Grant has just left, Papa, and the weather has turned terribly dangerous."

He joined her at the window, taking in the weather just as another flash of light and boom of thunder rattled the panes.

"Let us hope he returns home without injury. We'll send a stable hand over later today to ensure his safe arrival."

And just like that he was back again, his eyes clear of confusion. She bit her lip, wishing she knew what it was that ailed him so she may try to cure him of the disease.

"I think that would be best. I'll go and send word now to the stables. You may wish to ready yourself for luncheon, Papa. We'll be dining in an hour."

Clara walked from the room, and after telling the butler to send word to the stable, she was walking through the foyer about to head upstairs to change for lunch when the front door burst open and Mr. Grant stumbled in, water dripping from him as if he'd partaken in a swim since he'd left. He glanced at her, holding out his arms as if to stop his clothing from touching his sides.

"I do apologize, Lady Clara, but the causeway is flooded. It seems the storm hit upstream prior to hitting us here and I cannot make my way home."

Which was true, the Duke of Law's estate was in effect on a small island, surrounded by a river that when flooded made one housebound. She turned to the footman who looked at

Mr. Grant with annoyance that he was making a mess on the floor.

"Have the blue room prepared for Mr. Grant, and tell Mrs. Pennell there will be three for both lunch and dinner today."

"Yes, my lady."

"Follow me, Mr. Grant. I'll show you the room. The chambermaid will be up shortly to place fresh linens on the bed." Clara walked up the staircase, fully aware of the tall, dripping-wet man behind her. Her skin prickled in aware-ness and she had the oddest sense that he was staring at her neck. The urge to run her hand across her nape assailed her, but she did not. Not for a moment did she want him imag-ining he had any effect on her whatsoever.

For he did not, nor would he ever have.

She turned toward the guest wing of the house, pointing out rooms that he may wish to use should he need solitude. "With the river flooding you'll be here for some days. It's quite deep and rises quickly, but unfortunately does not go down as rapidly."

She opened a door halfway down the passage, swinging it wide. "This will be your room. It has a lovely view of the maze and has a desk, not that you'll be able to correspond with anyone at present, but even so…" What was she saying? She was blabbering like a nincompoop. "There is a dressing room through there," she said, pointing to a connecting door. "You may change in there. I'll have Papa's valet find some-thing to fit you and bring it in."

He threw her a tentative smile, running a hand through his thick, brown hair, pushing it off his face and for the first time in all the years she'd known Mr. Grant her stomach fluttered. "I'll instruct the maid to light the fire for you also. Is there anything else that you will need?" she asked with a sharp edge to her voice, annoyed to have reacted to him in such a manner.

He wiped a drop of water off his chin with the back of his hand and again her attention was seized. "No, thank you, Lady Clara. You're more than generous."

She turned without answer and walked from the room, before pausing at the threshold. "Well, I cannot have you stay in the stable. Father would never allow it." Clara walked away as fast as she could from the flash of disappointment she read in Mr. Grant's eyes at her words. She would not under any circumstance feel anything for him but contempt. He'd been rude and impolite to her during her first Season, which was unforgivable. That his sister stole her intended wasn't to be borne.

He was never your betrothed...in fact he never showed you that much interest.

She ignored the voice of reason and went downstairs to ensure everything was put in order for Mr. Grant before heading to her room where she found to her dismay that the rain had only grown stronger and now the wind had picked up. A day or two of Mr. Grant being at Chidding Hall may end up being a week.

Oh, however would she bear it?

👑

The following day Stephen sat in the upstairs parlor reading a book that the Duke had given him on the property he now leased. It was an interesting read and gave him more of an insight to his brother-in-law, the Marquess Graham, and his family on his grandmother's side.

The Duke seemed quite well today, bright and alert, and he was hopeful that maybe he would remain so, but after what Lady Clara had explained about his illness he doubted his day of clarity would last.

The door opened and a maid walked in, a few logs of wood in her arms. He stood, coming to her to take them. "Here, let me help you, miss."

She pulled them away, horror written on her face. "Oh no, my lord. I could not have you do that. I won't be a moment and I'll leave you in peace once again."

Stephen shook his head. "No, I insist. They look too heavy for you." He took them from her, surprised just how heavy they were when he grabbed them. He threw a couple of logs onto the fire before placing the others in the wood bin at the side of the fireplace. "I'm not a lord, merely Mr. Stephen Grant at your service."

The young maid grinned, a light blush stealing over her cheeks and he smiled in return. She was a pretty woman and the type of woman he'd always thought to marry one day. Before his sisters had married so very well and placed him in a precarious position. Related to people of high rank and yet without the funds to support such a lifestyle himself was oftentimes looked on with ridicule and pity. It was fortunate his brother-in-law was so very wealthy and could afford to lease him Ashby Cottage for a fraction of its worth.

"It's a pleasure to meet you, Mr. Grant. I'm Miss Daphne Smith."

The door opened and Lady Clara walked in. Her steps halted at the sight of them close before the fire and close enough to each other that to anyone it would look like a private tête-à-tête was at play.

She raised her brow and he knew what she was thinking. The chiding look she gave to Daphne was easy to read and the maid bobbed a quick curtsy before all but running from the room.

Stephen stared at Lady Clara in return and waited for the little minx to say something about his conduct.

She came farther into the room and sat over by the window, picking up a small basket he'd not seen there before, and pulling out a cushion that looked half completed along with needle and thread. "Cavorting with the help. I wondered how long it would be before you made trouble with one of our maids."

He sat, staring at the flames and counting to five before he answered, or stood and strangled the woman. "I was not cavorting, as you term it. I helped her with the wood for the fire and introduced myself. Had you found me making a beast with two backs you may have an issue to discuss."

She gasped, her needlework halted in her hands. "Have you forgotten whom you're speaking to? That rough, uneducated speech is not appropriate for a Duke's daughter. Mind your manners, Mr. Grant."

"Mind your own manners." He glared at the flames, his hands flexing in his lap. Out his peripheral vision he noticed she stood, hands on hips and he ground his teeth. Now he was in for a tongue-lashing.

"I do not need to mind my own manners, sir. I know very well what is expected of me and how to go about in this life. You will never see me cavorting with a footman or giving the staff hope of an understanding that is beyond their reach and too beneath mine. From when I was very little, Father has reminded me of my duty, of whom I should marry and why.

"You're now the brother of a marchioness and countess, being such one would think that you too would understand your limits. Not to mention you're a guest in someone else's home and should conduct yourself with respect and propriety. Seeing you with our maid does concern me as to how you get on in London at your sister's home."

Stephen stood, storming over to where Lady Clara waited near the window. Her eyes blazed with annoyance and something else he could not make out. Even so, he was glad she was mad, for it only matched his own ire.

"You have a sharp tongue. One day, Lady Clara, someone will tell you to keep it still in that pretty mouth of yours."

Her eyes widened and her mouth opened in a pretty little O. He clenched his jaw, willing himself not to look at her lips. *Don't do it, man, you'll regret it* a voice warned.

"And you, Mr. Grant should decide to which social sphere you wish to belong. This one you're now circulating in or the one you'll find below stairs."

"Jealous I was not talking to you instead of the maid? Maybe if I complimented your gown more often, or asked you to dance you would not be so bitter toward me."

She scoffed at his words but her cheeks pinkened, making her even more alluring than normal. When she was angry, she was like a hellcat protecting its kittens and he found it extremely alluring. "To be jealous one has to have emotions involved. When it comes to you, Mr. Grant, I do believe you think too highly of yourself. I do not care what you do outside of these walls, but in this house, you'll keep your hands off my staff."

"Has anyone ever told you how pompous you are? How judgmental and belittling you can be to those who are not of your rank? Do not forget the people belowstairs that you find so beneath your notice keep this house running and everyone in it fed, clothed and warm. What do you do, *Lady Clara*?" He accentuated her name, wanting to add a little sarcasm to his words.

Vexing chit!

"I pay their wage, that's what I do, Mr. Grant, which is more than you can say for yourself."

He took some calming breaths through his nose, sure he was breathing fire. How dare she, but then, how dare he? He was being unapologetically rude and he would not be surprised if she did make him sleep out in the stables.

"Really? Or does your father pay their wage?"

"I do, Mr. Grant," she retorted hotly. "My father no longer controls the finances or running of the estates. That has fallen to me and our steward since his health has declined."

The reminder that her father was ill, that she had multiple stresses on her small shoulders shamed him. He stepped back, turning away. "I think, Lady Clara, that we should part ways before any more is spoken and if at all possible, start our acquaintance again. I apologize for my conduct here this morning."

"Apology not accepted. You think me judgmental, and you too judge me and my friends. I've seen you in town, laughing, throwing us mocking looks whenever the chance arose. Do not think for a minute that I do not remember how rude you were to me in Hyde Park several years ago."

He scoffed. "I was rude. You were throwing yourself at my sister's husband. Do you think I would sit by and watch you shame her so? I will never allow anyone to treat my siblings such, not even a duke's daughter who was angry because the Marquess had not picked her."

"He had not picked your sister either, if I recall correctly." She stepped closer to him, the breath of her words fanning his ire even more. "Am I wrong, Mr. Grant? Was he not found in her room by mistake?"

"That is beside the point," he mumbled, knowing she spoke the truth. "Their marriage is a love match and a happy union. You shall not speak of Louise again. I'll not stand for it."

She laughed mockingly. "You will not stand for it. Really? And if I do, what do you plan to do? Chide me like a child?"

Right at this moment a good slap on her ass would do him a world of good. The thought of touching her derriere pulled him up short and he ran a hand over his jaw. He didn't want to touch her any more than she wanted to touch him. Did he?

"Take my words as the truth that they are. I'll not stand for you saying another word about my sisters."

Her eyes narrowed, and she glared at him as if he were the worst creature in England. Their breathing was ragged, and Stephen's attention snapped to her bosom that rose and fell with each of her breaths. He cursed the ample delights that sat nestled in her gown. She was not for him to ogle or think about in any other way than the annoying, rude Lady Clara that he'd forever dislike. Not for a moment would he think her strong-willed, defiant, beautiful...

"You do not tell me what to do. Ever." The last word accentuated with a step closer to his person, almost putting her breast-to-chest against him.

He did not move away, nor did she seem to realize just how close they were. He glared down at her plump mouth, pulled into a mocking smirk and something inside him snapped. She seemed to sense a change in him and her eyes widened, but still she did not scuttle away. Nor did he want her to. In fact, right at this moment all he could think about was kissing her within an inch of her life. Taking the maddening wench in his arms and seeing if her fire burned as bright in his arms as it did out of it.

Stephen reached for her, wrenching her from the short space that separated them and kissed her. His hand spiked into her soft curls and at her gasp, he deepened the kiss, thrusting his tongue against hers. She softened in his hold, her hands, tentative at first, clasped his shoulders before slipping about his neck.

She tasted like sweet tea and sin and he ravaged her

mouth, punished her for being so obstinate and alluring at the same time. Punished her for all the times he'd been on the receiving end of her wicked lips while drawing him ever closer. His body hardened and he hoisted her a little off her feet, holding her against his person. She melted against him, her body undulating against his and he hardened at the satisfied moan she expelled.

Footsteps sounded in the passage and they wrenched apart, putting much-needed distance between them.

"Ah, here you both are. I've been outside and the rain does not seem to want to relent." The Duke walked over to the window, staring out at the weather. "No, my opinion on this is correct. The rain is here to stay. You may be stuck with us, Mr. Grant, for several days at this point."

Lady Clara moved over to the window and picked up her sewing. Her lips were swollen and there was a pretty rose hue on her cheeks that he'd placed there. For a moment Stephen couldn't move. That kiss. *Shit!* He had not meant for that to happen, but now that it had, all he could think about was why the hell had the Duke picked that particular time to interrupt.

He inwardly groaned. For all that was holy, he needed help if he were thinking about Lady Clara Quinton in a romantic light. "I think you may be right, your Grace," he said, joining him at the window and looking out on the weather. "I hope you do not mind. My stay here was not purposefully done."

The Duke chuckled, waving his concerns away just as a muffled voice from behind him said, "I mind and the sooner you're gone the better."

He ignored her remark, making a note to take it up with her later. Or perhaps not. If he were tempted to kiss her again when they were alone it would probably be best if he stayed as far away from Lady Clara as much as possible until he could leave. If there was one thing he would promise himself, it would be to stay the hell away from her and the temptation she oozed.

She was not for him and he most certainly was not for her.

CHAPTER 5

*C*lara had managed to stay clear of Mr. Grant over the next day, but after dinner the following evening, her father had complained of a megrim and had retired to his room. She'd been unfortunate enough to have to retire to the drawing room after the meal where she was joined by Mr. Grant.

He sat across from her, lazily crossing his legs and lighting a cheroot. She sewed in her own chair, ignoring the heat that sizzled across her skin from his gaze. It traveled the length of her like a physical caress and she cursed him for tempting her so.

After their kiss the other day, her body had not been its usual, calm self. Her skin heated at the memory of his touch, the slide of his tongue against hers made her stomach clench and heat to pool at her core. Two things that never had occurred to her before. Not with anyone. When he'd wrenched her against him she had been tempted to claw at his face, and yet the moment his lips touched hers she was lost.

All thoughts of refusing him fled and instead she'd plastered herself against him as if her life were dependent on him holding her. She'd had the oddest sensations coursing through her blood, and her body ached in a way that instead of being painful was exciting, tempting, and something she wanted to do again.

How he must be congratulating himself on seducing her and making her jelly in his arms.

"Please can you do something else other than stare at me, Mr. Grant? I feel you inspecting me like some oddity on the street corner."

"You flatter yourself," he said, his voice flat and uninterested. Dismissive even. She hated when he spoke in such a way. Somehow it always made her feel unworthy. "Why would I stare at you? To do so would show an interest in the subject matter, which I do not have."

She ground her teeth. He was lying and she ought to call him out for such an untruth, but she could not. She was a lady after all, a duke's daughter. To call a gentleman out on his word was not the done thing. But his inspection of her was as true as the fact she was sitting across from him.

Her gaze flicked to the clock on the mantel.

"Trying to gauge if you've spent enough time with me?"

She shrugged, not willing to be polite if he was not. "You are right, which for you, Mr. Grant, must be a novel thing. It's not often I should imagine that you're right about anything."

He took a long draw of his cheroot before throwing it into the fire. He leaned forward, his elbows resting on his knees. "Do you want to know what else I'm right about, my lady?"

She shrugged again, curious and yet not. "I'm sure no matter what my reply, you're going to tell me anyway, so you may as well just get on with it."

Not that she wanted to know, for the amused gleam in his

eyes told her she would not like what he said. She had the oddest notion that he was laughing at her, or about to shock her. Which one it would be, she wasn't certain.

"That the kiss we shared made you as hot as it made me, and if I'm not mistaken, I would lay a gold sovereign on the table that it's all you've thought about since."

She stared at him, mouth agape before she closed it with a snap. Clara fought to find the words to tell him he was mistaken but they wouldn't come. Blast it. He was right of course. Every waking hour and sleep too she'd relived their embrace. His hands hard against her flesh, holding her against him as his mouth punished hers. What was wrong with her that she would be thinking of Mr. Grant, her enemy, in such a way? "How dare you be so crude."

"Am I wrong?" He lazed in his chair, his face suddenly serious, a dark, hungry glint in his eyes that made her stomach clench and her heart race.

"Yes, you're very wrong. I would rather kiss a fish than kiss you again."

"Liar."

She gasped, standing and throwing her sewing onto the floor. "Apologize or you will be removed to the stable like the common man who thinks he's speaking to a doxy instead of a lady."

He stood, striding over. Clara swallowed as he towered over her, his intense gaze, chiseled cheeks and full lips that she'd dreamed about last night staring down at her. Or more accurately, she'd dreamed about running her hands over those cheeks that were too perfect for a man. Of his mouth, soft and lush that had kissed her with such passion that she had woken up hot and flushed and aching in places she'd never ached before in her life except while in his arms. He was the devil's spawn. She hated him. Truly she did.

She did.

Didn't she?

"If I'm moved to the stable, you'll not be able to wield insults at me so easily. I would not deprive you of your sport, Lady Clara. I do believe you enjoy me."

Oh yes, she enjoyed him, that she knew with certainty. She'd enjoy having him touch her right now if only he would eliminate the need that coursed through her blood that only he seemed to evoke.

Blasted man.

"And you think I have a high opinion of myself. If I do, so do you, Mr. Grant."

He muttered something under his breath and clasped her face. Her hands came up to cover his, to remove his hold or keep him there she was not sure. The particulars did not matter, for within a moment he was kissing her again, and this time she met his tongue with hers, taking as much as he gave.

Clara ran her hands down his chest, the corded, strong muscles beneath her palms reminding her of what he looked like without his waistcoat and shirt. The thought did little to cool her desire.

He pulled back and she mewled in protest, having not had enough of his lips on hers. "You're too sweet. You should not taste as sweet as you do," he whispered.

Clara stared up at him as he watched her, his hands flexing on her hips and keeping her hard against him. "I dislike kissing you as well, Mr. Grant."

"Maddening chit." He kissed her again and she inwardly crowed. She'd never been kissed before Mr. Grant had moved into their home. His mouth moved on hers, drawing her ever closer. It was searing, wet and full of need. A real man's kiss that she'd only heard whispered about within the ballrooms of the *ton*.

Clara had always hoped to be kissed just so one day. So

passionately that all her troubles would melt away and all she would be left with was the moment of the kiss. One that consumed and inflamed her body and soul.

Mr. Grant's kiss did all of those things and more. How would she ever make him stop?

His hand dipped lower on her back and Clara found herself no longer in control of her body. Somewhere between the start of the embrace to this point her body had formed a mind of its own. It also seemed to know exactly what it wanted.

Him...

When his hand cupped her bottom, pulling her into his hardness, comprehension dawned of just where they were and who could walk in on them at any moment.

She wrenched from his arms, his eyes heavy-lidded with desire and dark with hunger. Clara held up a hand to warn him off, to keep him at bay when he reached for her again. "I do not know what just transpired between us, but it'll never happen again."

He wiped his bottom lip with his thumb, as if erasing all traces of her off his person. She didn't like that he did such a thing. Did he not enjoy their kiss? Was he laughing at her?

"It was merely a kiss, Lady Clara. Not much different to the one we shared two days ago." He studied her a moment and expectation rippled across her skin at the thought he was going to kiss her again. He seemed to rethink his choice and she chastised herself for the disappointment that shot through her blood. "It would be a shame in my estimation if it never happened again. I rather enjoyed our kiss, both of them."

She bit her lip at his words and a small flicker of pride filled her before she shook herself back to reality. They did not like each other and nor should they be doing anything together, other than tolerating each other's presence while Mr. Grant was a guest here.

"Goodnight, Mr. Grant." She started for the door, but he wrenched her back, tipping up her chin to look at her. Her body rioted for him to kiss her again. She tried to mask her desires, but at six and twenty, she found her emotions were not always so easy to conceal, to push down. Now that he'd kissed her, twice, her mind screamed to run, but her body wanted nothing more than to lean up against him like a cat against a person's leg and do it again.

"Goodnight, Lady Clara." He stared at her a moment and hope bloomed in her chest that he was about to kiss her again, but then he stepped back, clasping his arms about his back.

She left, not caring if her departure looked like a scuttle or even a slow run. To stay in his company, to want such a man, a man to kiss her again. One whom she had never liked only meant one thing... She was deprived of the company of the opposite sex, of men who were eligible to court a duke's daughter. Mr. Grant was not one of them.

What would her friends say if they knew she had been so intimate with Mr. Grant? They would laugh, think it a joke at first and then they would probably oust her from their set. For years she had taken great pains to let everyone know of her acquaintance that she disliked the Grants, Stephen and his social-climbing sisters. To kiss the man, to allow such intimacies went against everything that she stood for.

Clara made her room, shutting and locking her door before collapsing onto her bed. She frowned up at the ornate plaster ceiling. Worse was the fact that he kissed very well, not that she would ever tell him such a truth. He was kind to her father, did not amend His Grace's words when he made a mistake or did not remember what he'd said only five minutes before.

Had she been too quick to judge Mr. Grant? Had she been jealous that Miss Louise Grant married the Marquess Graham and she did not? She slapped the bedding at her side. Of course she'd been jealous, a raging lunatic if she remembered correctly. She could not have gone to any more trouble than she did during that Season to make Miss Grant feel unwelcome and friendless. Or her family.

She was a terrible person. After seeing the Marquess with Louise she knew that she never stood a chance of making him love her. He might not have known at the beginning of his marriage just how much he adored his wife, but it had become obvious quite quickly that he did. Seeing his lordship's affection had brought out the worst in Clara and Mr. Grant had been privy to most of her actions and caustic remarks over the fact.

It wasn't any wonder he loathed her for it.

With him staying here, and now after their two passionate encounters, it would only make the situation with him worse. She couldn't help but wonder if he'd kissed her to teach her a lesson, to tease her so he may use it against her when they were back in town.

Clara sat up on the bed and started unpinning her hair. She would not ring her maid, the last thing she wished for was company. When debating with oneself it was always better, in Clara's opinion, to do it in solitude. Then at least there was no one to tell you that you were a nincompoop and fool not just for one night, but for many years before.

CHAPTER 6

*C*lara jumped in her chair the following morning at breakfast when her father bellowed at the footman. "What are you looking at, boy? Do you think you can stare at me? The Duke of Law?"

Clara reached out a hand to clasp his and he pushed her away. He stood, his chair flying backward at his abrupt movement and she gazed up at him, not recognizing the wild, crazy man who stood before her. What was going on?

"Papa?" she said, trying to clasp his hand once again. He stared at her, his eyes wild and vacant and the flitting thought entered her mind that he did not know who she was. "Sit back down, Papa. Your breakfast is growing cold."

He stormed around the table and she squealed as she tried to get up off the chair. She wasn't quick enough and he grabbed her, clasping her arms in a vise-like grip, shaking her.

"Who are you, you wretch? You do not dine with the Duke of Law. Get below stairs where you belong."

"Father!" she yelled. "It's me, Clara."

The door opened and Mr. Grant strode in. His eyes flared

at the sight of what was going on and he stormed over to her, wrapping his arms about her father's and pulling him away.

"Your Grace, calm yourself." He pulled him back and Clara took a steadying breath, taking in the two footmen who stood idly by, their eyes wide with shock and their feet seemingly made of stone and not able to render assistance. "Leave us," she said, turning back to her papa, whom Mr. Grant still held and was edging back toward his chair.

"Father," she said again tentatively. "Do you know who I am?" Her eyes burned with unshed tears and she blinked to clear her vision, rummaging into her reticule for a handkerchief. Had he forgotten he had a daughter? If that were the case, she would have to ring for Dr. Miller and have him call on them as soon as the river dropped enough to be passable.

Her father's eyes cleared after a few minutes and Mr. Grant helped him to sit in his chair, kneeling beside him. "Your Grace, do you remember what just happened?"

Her papa rubbed a hand over his brow, frowning. "Did I spill the tea again, my dear?" he said to her, looking out over the breakfast table. "I do apologize if I did."

She smiled, although even to her it felt wobbly at best. "Are you feeling well, Papa? Would you like to lie down a moment?"

He nodded, not venturing to argue with her and that in itself was telling. Her father would never usually go back to his room throughout the day. He'd always been such an active, outdoors man. Loved to hunt, fish, ride his stallion. Whatever sickness that ailed him, it was only growing in severity. Mr. Grant helped him to stand and they walked him out into the foyer.

"I shall take the Duke to his room. Maybe you should see what the staff can do about getting word out to your family doctor so he may be ready to call when the river is passable."

Clara nodded, not bothering to reply, but simply going

straight to the housekeeper to give her instructions. Once she had ordered the servants to check on the river's height and prepare for Dr. Miller's arrival, she instructed Cook to make up a tisane and heat bricks for her father's bed since the weather had turned chill.

Clara walked back into the library, a sanctuary, a place that helped her remember that no matter what this issue with her papa's mind was, she would always have her memories of her father. Those at least could not be ripped from her.

"Lady Clara, are you well?" Mr. Grant walked into the room, coming over to her. For a moment she thought he may engulf her in his arms, but instead he looked about and then sat, staring up at her from the settee. He wrung his hands in his lap. "Your father is resting. Mrs. Pennell brought up a tisane that she said would calm him and make him sleepy."

Clara sat on a settee beside Mr. Grant, staring at her hands in her lap. "I've never seen Father so angry before. He's never raised his voice to his staff or myself. When he grabbed my arms it was like looking at a person whom I had never met." She took a calming breath, biting her lip to stop it from wobbling. "He's forgetting me," she said, meeting Mr. Grant's concerned gaze. "My papa is forgetting his daughter."

The tears did slip over her cheek at her words and she covered her face with her hands, lest he see her crying. A strong arm wrapped about her back and pulled her close. She went willingly, wanting the support, needing it more than she even knew. The horror of her father forgetting everything he'd ever been was too awful to face or accept.

He was forgetting her...

"I'm so sorry. I know this must be terribly hard for you."

Clara pulled back a little to stare up at him. What she found staring back at her gave her pause. She'd never seen Mr. Grant look at her with anything but loathing, or annoyance. Besides the two times they'd kissed, certainly he'd never shown a deeper emotion. His eyes were comforting, leaving her feeling warm and safe.

"Thank you for stepping in and assisting me. I could not manage to get Father to let me go and the footmen seemed to have been frozen from shock. That is twice you have rescued me. I will owe you a great debt by the time you leave for your own estate."

He rubbed her back, his thumb slowly working along her spine and making her skin prickle in awareness. The scent of sandalwood wafted from him, and she shut her eyes, liking that he smelled just as a man should, earthy and unpretentious.

"Has your father ever reacted like so before or is this a new development with his illness?"

"It's a new symptom and one that I never wish to see again. He was doing so well this morning, he sometimes does spill his tea or misses his mouth with his food or drink, but never has he ever forgotten who I am. Never has he become violent and grabbed me the way he did."

She looked up at him and met his eyes. "He's not getting any better, if anything he is getting worse every day. The decline has been so fast and now we're stuck here until I can get his London doctor out to see us."

Mr. Grant pushed back a lock of hair from her brow, placing it behind her ear. The action caused her to shiver. Of all the times she would react so to a man's touch, now was not the appropriate time to do it. But how could she not when it had only ever been Mr. Grant who made her feel alive, was not scared to chastise her when he thought she was being unfair? It had only ever been the man beside her that had caused her to react in any way.

"The river will go down in a day or so and then we shall fetch the doctor. I shall stay with you until his arrival to ensure you remain safe. Not that I think that your father would ever intentionally harm you, but that does not mean that he will not unintentionally hurt you and when he does realize his mistake, it would kill him to know you were injured. I will save you both from that pain at least."

"Thank you, Mr. Grant." She threw him a self-deprecating smile. "You are a better man than I gave you credit for, I'm afraid."

He grinned, tweaking her nose. "Well, the fault lies with me too. I have not been the kindest to you either, so I would think we're even in that regard."

♛

Stephen stared down at her and the warm coiling in his stomach started as she stared up at him with her injured, sad, blue eyes. He wanted to wrap her up in a protective shell and save her from this sadness, but he could not. Her father was ill, possibly gravely so, and he would stay by her side and see this sadness to its conclusion, which he'd started to think would end with the death of the Duke.

Not that he would tell lady Clara such a thing, but the decline from the Duke was startling and he could not help but think it would only get a lot worse before it ended.

A tear slipped from her eye and he wiped it away with his thumb. It was never pleasant to see a woman upset, even Lady Clara who had been his enemy for eight years or so. To see her in this situation showed him another side of her. A loving daughter, a daughter who was frightened and scared for her parent and heartbroken at the outcome she faced.

"Do not cry, my lady. Your father will have a rest and he should be back to rights this afternoon."

She shook her head, her hands holding fast against his chest. "I do not believe he will be. I have this terrible, sinking feeling that he's not long for this world. He's become so much worse. I thought bringing him home would be beneficial, and it was for a time, but now... His outburst at breakfast has never happened before. What if he starts to do this often? Whatever shall I do?"

He rubbed her back, trying to give as much comfort as he could. "I'll not leave you alone in this, and so whatever happens, we shall deal with it together. Agreed?" he asked, meeting her gaze.

She nodded, a small downward tilt to her lips. "Agreed."

CHAPTER 7

*T*he road to London and to Mr. Grant's estate became passable the following day. The family doctor was summoned from London and would now be on his way to Chidding Hall. Clara sat in a chair in the conservatory, a blanket over her legs as the day, although clear, was chill.

Mr. Grant had set off for his estate early this morning, but had promised to return this afternoon, with everything he would need to reside here for the duration of her father's illness. After her papa's outburst, his physical assault of her, something he'd never done in his life, Mr. Grant had decided to stay. Even as a child neither of her parents had laid a hand on her, so for him to shake her, his grip punishing and cruel had been out of character.

The tisane, whatever Mrs. Pennell had made up, worked wonders yesterday, and they had given more to her father today. He was sleeping, which under the circumstances was probably best.

Footsteps sounded on the tiled floor and she turned, placing the unread book in her lap aside. Pleasure and relief in equal values ran through her at the sight of Mr. Grant striding toward her. She'd never noticed his athleticism before, but how she did now. Not to mention their two kisses plagued her mind almost as much as her father did. What did it mean, their slip of etiquette?

Did it mean anything at all or was he simply so angry at her that he'd kissed her as further punishment? Not that it had been a punishment at all. The sweet words he'd breathed against her lips had not been a penalty to bear. They had sent her heart to pound and her body to want and need things she'd never known before in her life.

And now he was here to stay. However would she behave herself with him?

"Mr. Grant, you're back." He smiled and the breath in her lungs seized. When had he become so handsome? His wavy brown locks accentuated his chiseled cheekbones and strong jaw. His nose was perfectly straight, and his eyes, large and the kindest she'd ever seen, gleamed with pleasure. She could not recall thinking of him so fondly in London. Clara frowned as he came and sat beside her and he reached up and smoothed her brow with his thumb.

"Is something troubling you? Is everything well with your father this morning?"

She nodded, ignoring the fact that his touch did odd things to her. "He's asleep and better today. He ate breakfast in bed, but the tisane Mrs. Pennell made has put him to sleep."

Mr. Grant leaned back on the stone chair they sat upon, staring up at the sky through the glass roof. "The doctor should be here this afternoon and that should alleviate some of the pressures on you, Lady Clara." He turned and looked at her, his eyes skimming over her in appreciation. She'd seen that look before from other gentlemen in the *ton*, most especially Lord Peel, but with Mr. Grant bestowing such glances affected her like nothing she'd ever known.

"Please call me Clara, Mr. Grant. I think we're past correct forms of address after all that we've been through these past few days."

He grinned and she had to look away lest she lean over, clasp him by his too-good-looking jaw and kiss him again. "This is where you may say in return that I may call you by your given name too."

He chuckled, leaning toward her and with one finger tilted up her chin. "You may call me Stephen, Clara."

Her name was but a whisper and she swallowed, biting her lip at the gravelly, deep voice in which he'd said her name. Never had her name sounded so evocative or, dare she say it, sensual before in her life.

"Stephen," she whispered, but even to her own ears it sounded like a plea. No doubt he heard the need, the want in her tone and without further prompting, he closed the space between them and kissed her.

Clara sighed at the rightness of having him in her arms once again, clasping his nape and kissing him back. His hair was soft under her gloveless fingers, his skin warm. He licked her bottom lip and she gasped as he deepened the kiss. His mouth covered hers with delicious wantonness and she could not get enough. For a man that she'd once reviled she certainly enjoyed his kisses.

She could no longer say that about Stephen, that she disliked him. Over the last few days he'd shown a side of himself as loyal and kind toward those in need. She supposed the night he'd helped her in Covent Garden she should have recognized that trait of his, a caring nature. With her, here and alone he was different. Gone were the harsh looks, the dismissing words whenever they had interacted. The man kissing her now could not be more different and she could not be more changed too, since seeing this side of him.

"I should not be kissing you like this." He leaned his forehead against hers, holding her gaze. "We're enemies, are we not?"

Clara clasped his jaw, kissing him quickly before pulling back. He let her go, but he watched her, his eyes wary and curious as to what she was going to say. "We are, or at least, we always have been in the past."

He leaned back in the chair, a small smile playing about his very kissable mouth. "Whatever we are, I will tell you this truth, Lady Clara. I enjoy your kisses and would welcome more of them from you if you were in agreement."

Heat bloomed on her cheeks and she bit her lip, not sure where to look at Stephen's words. She enjoyed his kisses as well, more than she ever thought she would, but what then? She was a duke's daughter, expected to marry someone of equal rank to her. Mr. Grant was only circulating in their social sphere due to whom his sisters had married. Kissing him could not lead anywhere. But it did not mean they could not enjoy this time together while he was a guest here at Chidding Hall.

A little doubt niggled at her conscience that she should not give him false hope that their newfound intimacies would lead anywhere permanent, but she also did not want to lose him. His support, protection and help in regard to her father. It was a selfish thought, but she had no one else. As an only daughter, there were no siblings to call on, she had no cousins, aunts, or uncles. Her father was all she had, and now Mr. Grant, who offered to help. She would not throw away such support, not for anything, not even the little guilt that taunted her that she was being unfair.

"I am in agreement," she said, sliding over to lean on his chest. "As strange and new as all of this is to me, I'm glad that you're here. Thank you for your support with my father. I'll forever be grateful."

He pushed a lock of hair from her face, his thumb tracing down her cheek to run across her bottom lip. "The first time that I saw you in London I will admit to being a little taken aback at your beauty. Your golden locks, perfectly coiled atop your head most days, your brows," he said tracing one, "a faultless outline to the bluest eyes I'd ever seen. From across the room those eight years ago, I knew they were the color of a tempestuous ocean after a storm." He chuckled a little. "Little did I know just how wild a storm you would be."

Clara swallowed the lump in her throat at Stephen's words. No one had ever complimented her in such detail before. Oh, she'd had compliments on how pretty she looked, what a lovely gown, her perfect smile, but no one, not even her father, had ever explained in such detail her features and no admirer had ever said that when they had seen her for the first time that they had been taken aback, dazed into staring and taking their fill.

Which was what Mr. Grant had seemed to do.

"And then I ruined your illusion by opening my mouth and putting you in your place, if I recall."

He shook his head, frowning. "If I remember correctly, the first time we spoke it was I who put you back in your place for being rude to my sister."

Clara laid her head against his shoulder. His arm wrapped about her back and held her against him. "Please know that I am very happy for your sisters and their marriages. I will admit to being injured by Marquess Graham, that I hoped and thought his courting of me would lead to marriage. I suppose I did not take my ire out on his lordship and rather redirected it at your sister." She looked up at him and met his surprised visage. "I will apologize to her the next time I see her."

"She would like that very much. Louise is not the type of woman who likes to have enemies. I think if she could, she would enjoy having you as a friend, and I think you, Clara, could do with a friend who was honest and loyal."

She sighed. How true that was. Her friends in London were as fickle as they came. Most of them had married now, some were even parents of small children, but still they gossiped, made fun of debutantes who were less fortunate in looks or stature than themselves. They flirted and teased each other's husbands to the point where Clara had wondered if some of her friends were having rendezvous outside the marriage bed. Stephen was steadfast, loyal, and something told her his sisters would be as well. In the future she may need that sort of support if her father continued to decline and she was left with no one.

"I will make amends, I promise." She closed her eyes, lulled by the sound of his heart beating under her ear. How was it that in only a short time she'd become so very comfortable around him? The comforting thought was her last before sleep enfolded her.

👑

Stephen had Lady Clara's maid pull back her bedding so he may place her on the crisp, clean sheets. He'd allowed her to sleep against his person for some time in the conservatory, before he realized that his back would cramp if he stayed in the position for too much longer. Even though it was not yet luncheon, Clara had a lot on her mind of late, so many worries and responsibilities it was only probable that she was exhausted. Caring for the Duke and the ducal properties would not be easy and would be time-consuming.

He headed back downstairs to the library. He would read

for a time before the doctor arrived, which should be early this evening if his calculations of travel were correct.

At some point he too fell asleep and only woke to the sound of voices in the foyer, one of those a man's and Clara's, who was greeting the guest. Stephen rose quickly, checking his cravat and sliding on his coat as he stepped out into the foyer.

Clara spotted him, and turned the older gentleman his way. "Dr. Miller, this is Mr. Grant. He was unfortunately waylaid here for some days due to the river coming down and has been helping me with Papa. As I stated in my letter to you, it was Mr. Grant who stopped father from shaking me."

The doctor shook his hand. "Good to meet you, Mr. Grant, and thank you for your time here assisting Lady Clara. It is most appreciated, I'm sure. Now, shall we go upstairs and see his Grace?"

"Yes, this way if you please, Dr. Miller."

Stephen followed and stood at the back of the ducal suite as the doctor went about his inspection of the Duke, who was awake and sitting up in bed, his discarded mail on the bedside cupboard.

The doctor did what looked like a few tests with the Duke's hands, reactions, and then he spoke to him at length, questioning him about all sorts of subjects that Stephen wondered whatever had to do with anything. Even so, the doctor continued, before showing Lady Clara a vial of liquid that was to be added to his tea every morning. "Shall we discuss this further in the library, Lady Clara? I would welcome refreshments if it's not too much trouble," the doctor said, standing.

"Of course," Lady Clara said, settling her father before leaving the room. They headed down to the library. Clara rang for tea and biscuits, notifying the staff that there would be an extra guest for dinner and to prepare a guest chamber.

During the time the tea was being prepared they spoke very little about the Duke. When a footman brought in the tea and Clara asked for them not to be disturbed, only then did the doctor explain his findings.

"Regarding your father," he said, placing down his cup and saucer after taking a sip. "I do not have good news, Lady Clara. In the few weeks that you've been home I can see a marked decline in his cognitive ability and there is a slight tremor affecting his hands that you may not have noticed. In London I was not certain the Duke suffered from the affliction that I'd seen before, but upon inspecting him again today, I fear that he does indeed have a similar disease I've seen in only a few of my patients in the past. I'm so very sorry, my dear, to be the one to tell you this, but he will not survive its progress."

Stephen moved over to sit beside Clara, taking her ice-cold hand. He rubbed it, trying to force warmth into her body, but she was silent and still, shocked he had no doubt.

"My father is dying?" she asked at length, her voice almost inaudible.

The doctor nodded, reaching out to squeeze her arm. "I'm sorry, my lady. You must prepare yourself for the progression of the disease to strip your father of who he once was. He will forget how to do things for himself, he may become angry and upset and be quite pleasant on other occasions. His food will need to be cut up in smaller portions for him so he will not choke and I would suggest that you do not let him wander about alone. He may become disoriented and lost. He will become a danger to himself and I would suggest the hiring of a caregiver. I have one whom I can suggest and write to if you approve."

She did not answer and Stephen met the doctor's eyes. "Thank you, Dr. Miller. That would be most kind."

The doctor's attention turned back to Clara, concern in his gray orbs.

"Is there anyone we can summon to help you? Family or friends you may want here, my lady?" Stephen asked, holding her hand and hoping the terrible gray pallor of her skin would go away.

She shook her head and his heart broke at the sight of the unshed tears welling within her blue eyes. "I do not have anyone. Father is all I have, Stephen."

He pulled her into his arms, holding her tight as she succumbed to her tears, her body shaking in his hold.

"Do you have any idea, Dr. Miller, how long his Grace may have left?" Stephen did not really want to know, but with Clara as upset as she was, he doubted she would remember to ask such a question, and yet it was be something she would want to know. His surmise was right as she lifted her head, dabbing at her cheeks with the back of her hand.

"Dr. Miller?" she queried. "How long did your other patients have before the end?"

The doctor looked down at his hands clasped in his lap, his knuckles white. "Your father seems to be nearing the end stage of the disease. I would surmise three months if you are lucky, one if you're not."

Clara gasped, her face draining of color altogether.

"It is a shock, my dear. I know, but I would suggest you take this time to spend it with your father as best as you can. Try to keep a brave face in front of him, take him out on picnics or rides in the carriage, just be certain to have his caregiver or Mr. Grant with you at all times. The medication I gave to you will help calm him when the need arises. Give it to him in the morning and then he should be quite manageable during the day. When he no longer is, you know your time is limited."

"Thank you, Dr. Miller," she whispered, clutching at Stephen's hand. "I will make the most of the time I have left with Papa."

CHAPTER 8

*C*lara had adhered to her promise to Dr. Miller over the next month and a half. They had made day trips to their neighbors, taken tea and cakes out in the woods surrounding the ducal property. At one point even a deer had walked up uncommonly close to them as they sat and ate. Her father had smiled and laughed at the brazen animal and the day had been one to remember.

Stephen had stayed at the estate during the entirety of her father's illness, helping the caregiver Dr. Miller had sent to them from London and being of any assistance he could. The man had done everything for the Duke that Clara could not do herself and she would be forever grateful for making her father's last few weeks comfortable and pain-free.

A quick rap upon her door pulled her from her sleep and she sat up so quickly the room spun a little.

"Who is it?" she asked

"Lady Clara, it's me, James. You need to come to the Duke's room. Straightaway, my lady."

Before her father's valet's words had stopped she was out

of bed and wrapping a shawl about her shoulders. She ran from the room to her father's. He lay still on his bed.

"He is unresponsive, my lady," the doctor stated, checking her father's pulse. "I cannot wake him."

"Father," she said, getting up on the bed to sit beside him. He had grown frail and much older than his fifty-four years during the past month and she was certain that if he were to walk into a London ballroom the *ton* would not recognize him today. "Papa, please wake up." Tears welled in her eyes, and she ran her hands over his cheeks, shaking him a little. "Papa…please, please don't leave me alone."

Her father opened his eyes, meeting hers and hope bloomed in her chest. He gave her a tired, little smile and her heart broke. She was losing him. Her only family and he was going away. "I will never leave you, my darling. I will always be with you. In here," he said, lifting his hand and pointing at her heart.

She nodded and tried to smile, but even to her it felt wobbly and uncertain. "I love you," she said, unable to stop the tears or the sob that escaped in front of all who stood behind her, Stephen included.

"The moment you were born you were the love of my life, my child. I'm proud of you, my dear."

She hugged him, holding him close as the last of his worldly breath left his body. The comforting hand of Stephen's slid over her back, stroking and supporting her in this time.

How would she ever survive without her father and Stephen, who too now would be going back to his estate? The realization made her heart ache even more and her chest burned as if she could not get enough air. She was going to be alone, an unmarried woman without a protector, without any family. Tears slid freely down her cheeks. However would she manage?

ive days later she stood in the drawing room downstairs after having laid to rest her father in the family mausoleum. All of London looked to be in the room, her friends and their husbands had made the journey from London, including Lord Peel. The gentleman whom she had not seen since Covent Garden stood to the side of the room watching her as if she were a juicy piece of meat that his wolfish teeth wanted to rip apart.

Her childhood friend Julia, now Lady Davenport after marrying the Earl Davenport, sidled up to her, her face animated as if she were enjoying an evening out at a ball, not having just buried her friend's father.

"I suppose you'll be in mourning now for several months. How droll that will be. I will not mourn my own papa when he passes. I do not think he ever cared for me at all, certainly not enough to stop me from marrying Lord Davenport who is as droll as they come." Julia smiled, looking about the room. "Not that you will have any troubles finding a husband of considerable worth. Lord Peel is still interested if his fixation on you is any indication."

Clara glanced in Lord Peel's direction and watched as he saluted her with his glass of whisky. She looked elsewhere, anywhere but him, and found her attention locked on Mr. Grant who spoke to his sister and the Marquess who had arrived yesterday at his estate, or so he had said. The Marquess owning the estate adjacent to this one, and having been their neighbor in the past, thought it only right to pay his last respects to her father.

"I'm not interested in Lord Peel or anyone at present." She finished her glass of wine and summoned a footman for another. Not that that was entirely true, she was interested in someone, but that someone was not titled, not a land owner, not in his own right at least. As a duke's daughter there were expectations required of her, expected from her. Mr. Grant did not suit those requirements. He was, however, the only man whom she'd ever wanted in a physical sense, not to mention an intellectual one as well. "I will return to town for next year's Season and not before. Only then will I decide what I shall do regarding a husband."

"Oh my, would you look who is in attendance? That gauche family, the Grants. I see Mr. Grant and his sister still think that they are welcome at such events."

Clara shushed her friend, looking about to ensure no one had heard her unkind words. "Remember this is my father's funeral. If you would show a little respect for me and my guests, I would be thankful. You may say whatever you wish in London, but not here. Not today."

Julia raised her brow, her lips puckering into a displeased mien, but Clara did not care. She was not in the mood for petty hate, and derogatory references toward a man whom she had come to admire, depend upon and like.

She met his eyes across the room and her heart missed a beat. He threw her a knowing smile, and she could not stop the one he brought forth on her lips. How sweet he was, how kind and patient he'd been toward her and her many tears over the past month. Her father's ups and downs that had occurred due to the disease that wrecked his body and left him nothing like the man she'd once known. Stephen had been beside her the whole time, keeping her will strong and comforting her when needed.

He had not tried to kiss her again, although there were many times she'd wanted him to. She longed for the comfort of him, wanted to feel anything but the severing pain she always felt when around her papa. Now that her father was gone, what was she going to do? There was time to make a decision, but no matter how much time passed it would not change that Clara's social stature was so very different to Stephen's.

Not that she imagined he thought of her as his future wife, he'd certainly never brought up such subjects with her, but she could not help but wonder if he contemplated such things when alone.

"Lady Clara," Lord Peel said, bending over her hand and bringing it to his lips. "May I say how very sorry I am for the loss of your father, the Duke. He was a great man and well loved."

"Thank you," Clara said, pulling her hand away. "It is very nice to see so many of his friends and acquaintances here today." Not that Lord Peel had ever been friends with her papa. In fact, her father had disliked the man, long before he started showing a marked interest in Clara. She supposed now having learned more of Lord Peel and his inappropriate actions toward women when defenseless she could understand why her father had never offered friendship. Perhaps her father had known somehow of his ungentlemanly ways with the fairer sex.

"We will be sad not to see you in town, but I heard you say to Lady Davenport," he said, bowing to Julia who still stood beside her, listening to the conversation, "that you will return next Season. I shall count the days until we see you again."

She would not count the days...

She nodded, not the least thrilled about such an outcome. "I should probably greet Papa's friends before they start to leave. If you'll excuse me." Clara started when Lord Peel took her arm, guiding her about the room.

"Allow me, my lady. I shall escort you."

Clara took a calming breath, ready to tell the gentleman that she did not need or want his type of support. His touch made her skin crawl and she could not help but marvel at how different she was when around Lord Peel than Mr. Grant.

"Lady Clara," Stephen said, bowing in front of her and holding out his arm. "I will escort Lady Clara about the room, Lord Peel. No need to trouble yourself." Clara pulled her arm free from Lord Peel's and placed it on Stephen's, turning quickly to thank his lordship for his help. "Thank you, my lord for your kind words. If you'll excuse me."

She ignored the glare that passed between the two gentlemen and allowed Stephen to guide her about the room to talk to her guests. "Thank you for removing me from his lordship. I did not ask for him to assist me."

"I gathered as much. His marked interest in you today is as forward and telling as it was in London. Be wary of him, my lady. I do not trust him to act honorably in his pursuit of you."

"What do you mean?" she asked, glancing up at him.

"Only that he's cornered you once alone already and would have done who knows what had I not heard your calls. I would not trust him not to try such things again."

"And I'm alone now. With father gone, maybe I should hire a companion again."

"I think that would be best, but you're not alone. I'm here, and I will be only next door should you need me."

She clutched at his arm, hugging it a little. "Thank you for all you've done these past weeks. I do not know what I would have done without you. You keep surprising me, Mr. Grant. I fear that we'll soon have to admit that we're friends."

He chuckled, the sound low and honeyed. It did odd things to her nerves. "I think we might. How terribly boring. I kind of enjoyed our verbal fisticuffs. Did you not?"

"I may have, but I do enjoy this kind of verbal discourse more." Clara tore her gaze from his before anyone noticed that they were both staring at each other, close and quite comfortable in each other's company. "How long are the Marquess and Lady Graham staying at Ashby Cottage?"

"They leave tomorrow. Will you dine with us tonight? I do not like the thought of you here alone."

She shook her head. "Thank you for your kind offer, but no. I feel tonight I want to be alone. Once everyone has gone, I shall retire early. I feel very weary all of a sudden. I think the past weeks have caught up with me."

"Very well," he said, patting her hand that sat atop his arm. "I will not push you to attend, but know, no matter the time or weather, should you need me, I will come."

"Thank you, Mr. Grant. I do not know what I would have done without you."

"You would have done exactly what I expected. You would have managed just as well as you did with me here. If there is one thing I know about you, Lady Clara, you're a strong woman, independent and loyal. Admirable qualities all. I'm in awe of you."

Clara blinked back tears, biting her lip to stop herself from crying in front of everyone. "Will you call tomorrow?"

"I will call as soon as my guests depart."

CHAPTER 9

*C*lara could not sleep. She tossed and turned, rolled about on her bed, but in no way could she find a position that was comfortable. This was the first night that Stephen was not under the same roof as her, and she disliked the idea of being all alone, save her servants.

She glanced at her windows, the heavy damask curtains pulled closed on the cold, fall winds that had picked up in the afternoon. A howling could be heard from outdoors and even though she told herself it was just the wind against the house, she struggled not to clutch her bedding as if it would save her from some otherworldly ghoul.

Clara threw back her blankets and strode over to the fire, throwing a piece of wood onto the dying embers. She reached up on the mantel and lit a candle using the hot coals before going about her room and lighting the others.

She sat before the hearth, reaching out her hands to warm them, her mind consumed with thoughts of Stephen. There was little use in denying that she had emotions invested in the man, more than she should ever have allowed herself.

He was everything she wanted in a husband—he was

kind, loving, caring and passionate. Certainly her every reaction to him had been telling, had told her more than once that he brought forth in her a passion she'd never had before. He spoke to her as an equal, did not dismiss or belittle her because she was a woman.

The wood caught alight and she watched as the flames licked at the wood, charring it. If only he were not so beneath her in rank. Should he be her equal in rank, fortune and property, he would have suited her in all ways, but she could not ignore the fact that he was not such things. That is was she who would bring the wealth and position to a union and she could not help but fear that somewhere, deep down inside, that was the reason for his liking her. Other gentlemen had certainly made it plainly obvious she was most sought-after because she was an heiress, but that wasn't enough.

She wanted a husband who loved her, not her money. If she married a man of wealth and position there would be no question as to why he wanted her for his wife. It would be because he cared for and loved her.

To marry someone out of that sphere would be a gamble and one she was not sure she could take.

A light knock sounded on the door and she started, holding still, unsure that she'd heard what she thought she did.

"Clara," a masculine voice whispered. "Clara, are you awake?"

Stephen? She stared at the door as nerves took flight in her stomach. He was here? Now? In the middle of the night…

She walked to the door and opened it. There, standing before her in nothing but breeches and a shirt and greatcoat was Mr. Grant. He was damp from the weather outside, and his hair was windblown, no doubt from riding his horse across the fields to Chidding Hall from Ashby Cottage.

"What are you doing here?" She glanced out into the passage and seeing no one about, pulled him into her room. "How did you get in?"

"The footman assumed I was still staying here and I didn't correct him on that assumption." He walked over to the fire and stood, warming his back. "I couldn't sleep."

"Neither could I," she said, going over to him. She had not thought to see him again today, but now with him before her, she was glad of it. In the few hours since he'd been here, she had missed him and that in itself was troubling. She wasn't certain what to do, or how their relationship would carry on now that her father had passed. All that she knew was that she liked Stephen and desired him more than anyone ever in her life.

He looked down at her, his eyes stealing over her and her lack of attire. She was dressed in her nightgown and little else and heat crawled over her face that he was seeing her thus.

"You should probably leave, Stephen," she said, not meaning a word she spoke.

His gaze heated and he reached out, running a finger along the lace collar of her nightdress. "Is that what you want?"

No. "Yes," she breathed as his hand slid farther down on her person to run along the flesh of her breast. Heat pooled at her core and she swallowed a moan when his hand flexed and he cupped her breast fully.

He followed his hands with his lips and she didn't stop him. Clara shut her eyes, clasping the nape of his neck as his tongue came out to flick her nipple. A shock ran through her at his touch and she was powerless to stop what was happening between them.

How could she halt this interaction that she'd wanted for so long now? With every kiss they shared, every look and touch over the past weeks she'd wanted him to do more. Now that he was, she was not about to stop him.

He moved and kissed her other breast and she moaned her acquiescence. His mouth was hot, wet and teased her with little licks of his tongue and full mouth kisses. Liquid heat pooled between her legs and she squeezed them together to try to quell the need that thrummed there.

Before she knew what was happening, he scooped her up in his arms and strode for the bed, throwing her onto the covers. Clara chuckled as she bounced before she watched in fascination as Stephen ripped his breeches buttons open and pushed them off his legs. His greatcoat, cravat and shirt soon followed and within a minute he was standing before her, as naked as Adam was with Eve.

Clara's mouth dried at the sight of him and she licked her parched lips, wanting to feel those corded muscles against her, pushing her down and taking her as she'd longed for him to for weeks now. His eyes darkened with hunger and she shivered, fully aware that she was still dressed in her nightgown.

"Take it off, my lady."

At his deep, rough command she did as he asked without question. At this moment in time she would do whatever he wanted of her so long as he touched her again. He reached down and took himself into his own hands, stroking his manhood until it jutted out before him.

Clara kneeled on the bed and wrenched the gown from her body, leaving her as bare as he was before lying back down. He kneeled on the bed, kissing his way up her body before settling between her legs. So many emotions rioted through her blood that she did not know what to do, but she could feel. Her body hummed with a need that she'd not known before, and all she craved was for him to take her. Make love to her.

"You're so beautiful," he whispered against her lips before kissing her with an unhurried air. He rocked against her core, making her gasp and she lifted her legs, hooking them about his waist.

"You're teasing me," she moaned when he nipped her neck before licking it better.

"I'm teasing us both."

Clara ran her hands over his back, feeling the corded muscle that ran down his spine. It flexed with each rock against her and she reached farther to clasp one perfect bottom cheek in her hand, pulling him against her. "Enough, Stephen. I want you," she demanded.

His hot breaths mingled with hers and he met her gaze as he reached down between them, placing his manhood at her core. And then, inch by delicious inch he slid into her. She gasped as pain ripped, stinging at where they joined. He stilled, kissing her lips, her cheeks and neck.

"I'm sorry, my darling. I did not mean to hurt you."

Clara shook her head, taking in this new feeling of him between her legs, the fullness and strangeness of being with a man for the first time. He felt too large, too wide and hard to go any farther, but then he rocked slowly forward and there was no pain, only pleasure and a throbbing ache that would not abate.

"Don't stop," she managed to say, liking the feel of his chest as it grazed hers with each thrust. She undulated beneath him, wanting more. There was no longer any friction, only pleasure, and Clara let herself go, to enjoy all that he could give her, tonight at least.

*S*tephen thrust into Clara, taking her as he'd dreamed of from the very first moment they kissed. She was so hot and wet, and clamped about his cock with a force that left him breathless and struggling not to spill too soon.

He needed her to climax, he had to make this night as enjoyable for her as it would be for him. It had, however, been quite some months since he'd slept with a woman and it was taking all the control not to climax like a green lad of eighteen.

Her fingers spiked into his back, drawing him close and he gave her what she wanted, thrust deep and hard into her willing heat. She threw back her head, gasping, and he kissed her neck, savoring her sweet perfume of jasmine as he pumped over and over into her.

Their breaths mingled, their hearts thrummed loud enough that he was sure he could hear them. Her legs rode high on his hips and he reached down with one hand, holding her ass as he took her.

"Oh yes," she panted, her eyes fluttering closed. "Stephen..."

Their actions were frantic as he pushed her ever closer to release and then he felt it, the small and then large tremors that thrummed through her core, dragging him along to climax. He pumped hard and deep, and she screamed, thrusting her hands above her head to push against the head-board as he fucked her without remorse.

For a moment he stayed in her, sweat covered their skin as he regained his breath and wits. Never before had he ever felt the way he felt with Clara. He flopped beside her, pulling her into the crook of his arm. Idly, he played with her hair, sliding it off her damp forehead.

"I hope I did not hurt you."

She rolled against him, laying her hand across his stomach to play with his ribs. "Oh no, you did not hurt me at all. In fact," she said reaching down to take his semi-hard phallus in her hand, "it only makes me more curious about what else a man and woman can do. Our first encounter was quite enjoyable."

He chuckled at her mischievous grin. "Lady Clara, you're a vixen."

She leaned over and flicked his nipple with her tongue, eliminating the concept of giving her time to recover from their first bout of lovemaking. He'd take her all night if she allowed it. "Only with you, Mr. Grant," she replied, doing it again and making his morals fuzzy. "Now, show me more."

Stephen groaned, and yet, was only too happy to oblige her ladyship. "Of course. Let us begin…"

CHAPTER 10

Stephen arrived at Lady Clara's estate just after luncheon the following day and found her behind her father's desk in the library, a pile of missives and scrolls lying before her. She glanced up at him, pleasure written on her features when she saw him.

"Stephen, you've arrived at the most opportune time. Please take me away from all this work." She stood and came around the desk and walked to the bell pull on the mantel, ringing for a servant. "Shall we have tea?"

"Yes," he said, seating himself beside her and kissing her quickly. "How are you today? You look like you're very busy."

"Father's lawyers have left some estate paperwork for me, along with his will that they read here yesterday. I'm trying to take everything in that has fallen on my shoulders and catch up with correspondence that had arrived during father's illness. I think it will take me some weeks to get through it all."

Stephen glanced at the desk. There was certainly quite a lot of papers to sort through. "When do you have to leave to make way for the new Duke of Law?"

She frowned, leaning back into the sofa. "I do not have to make way for anyone. The house and most of Papa's properties were not entailed. Father's family had a modest Tudor estate several miles from here that comes with the duchy, but this estate was owned by my mother's family. It was my great-grandmother's ancestral home and is handed down to the eldest daughter. We've always lived here as father preferred it to his own modest estate. So I do not have to go anywhere." She threw him an amused grin. "Are you sick of being my neighbor already, Mr. Grant?"

He shook his head. "No, never." He took in what she said and what it meant. She was an heiress, that he always had known, but now, the land and estates she must own, well, it placed her far above his expectations, his abilities to court a woman of such high rank. Disappointment stabbed at him that he could not be what society expected Clara's husband to be.

There was a light knock at the door before a footman came in carrying a tea tray. He placed it before them, then stood to the side. "Lady Clara, a Lord Peel is here to see you. He waits in the foyer."

Clara's eyes widened, and he noted the flicker of fear that entered her blue orbs. She glanced at him, and he squeezed her hand. "If you wish it, I will not leave you while you're speaking with his lordship." Although what Lord Peel needed to say to Clara, Stephen couldn't fathom. The man should return to London and stay there. He'd thought he already had, but even now that fiend loitered about Kent and near Clara.

"Show him in." She adjusted her seat and Stephen stood, positioning himself before the fire to await his lordship's entry.

They did not have to wait long before the strutting

peacock walked into the room and stopped at the sight of Stephen.

"Mr. Grant. I did not expect to find you here." Lord Peel pulled off his hat and gloves, handing them to the footman who hovered nearby.

"I'm taking tea with Lady Clara."

His lordship came and without waiting for Clara to say anything, sat himself beside her. He poured himself a cup, thereby leaving Stephen without one. "I wished to call and to ensure that you are well, my lady. You have had a terrible personal blow and I wanted to show that you have my support in any way you choose."

Stephen raised his brow. *I bet she does, you cad!*

"Thank you, my lord. That is very kind." She poured herself a cup of tea, and for a moment Stephen watched as they enjoyed their repast. "What brings you back here, my lord? I thought everyone had returned to town."

"To offer my condolences once again, and to see that you have everything in hand. In times like these, please feel free to use my expertise in relation to running estates, investments, servants' salaries and such. I'm more than capable in running multiple properties, which you, with your delicate constitution, will not be."

Stephen masked his chuckle with a cough at his lordship's words. Delicate constitution... Was the man blind to her annoyance or simply too dumb to realize it? Either way Clara nodded as if his lordship spoke the truth and her mask of indifference did not slip.

"All is in hand, my lord. Anything that I find challenging I have my father's steward to guide me."

He reached out and patted her hand and Stephen glared at where he made contact with her. He didn't want Lord Peel or anyone touching one piece of her if he could help it. He stilled at his own thoughts. When had he become so possessive of her? When had he started to think of her as his and no one else's? He supposed their coming together a night past had something to do with it, but also over the last month of seeing her battle against her father's illness, seeing a vulnerable side of Clara, his heart had softened toward a woman he'd once thought the spawn of the devil.

"Mr. Grant has been a great help these past weeks. In the ones to follow I'm sure all will work out. He's my neighbor if you do not know, Lord Peel."

Lord Peel scoffed and, finishing his cup of tea, placed it on the small table before them. "Is that what you aspire to be, Mr. Grant? A steward, a bookkeeper for a great house such as this one? I'm sure I can ask around London and see if any of my friends are looking for a new employee in that field."

Stephen narrowed his eyes on the viscount, well aware of the game he played. He wanted Lady Clara for himself, that he'd known for some months, but to treat him with so little respect, to mark him as a person beneath the *ton's* notice would not be tolerated.

"I've leased Marquess Graham's estate and so I'm not in need of a steward. I have hired one already." Of course he would have preferred to have not had to rely on his brother-in-law's charity to enable him to make something of himself. What man did not want to become successful in his own right? But unlike Lord Peel, not everyone was born with a silver spoon in their mouth.

The Marquess may have enabled him to live the life which he now did. Had bestowed on both him and his sister Sophie a small sum of money, but it was not enough to keep him forever without occupation.

To keep the lifestyle he now lived, he would have to work the land, budget and run the estate as well as any high-born lord would.

"Yes," Lord Peel said, rubbing his jaw as if he'd spied a

delicious sweet. "I heard the Marquess had leased the property to you, and for a fraction of what it was worth. I should imagine no respectable man would accept such charity. You are obviously not such a man."

Lady Clara stood, coming to stand beside him. "Thank you for coming, Lord Peel, but I think it's time you leave."

His lordship stood, adjusting his cravat. "I do apologize, Lady Clara, but as an equal I feel it is my duty to remind you and warn you of those who would take advantage of your sadness. Other than his sisters' exalted marriages, we know nothing of Mr. Grant. He may be a charlatan for all we know."

"Would my fist in your face make us better acquainted, my lord? I can certainly bestow you the honor if you choose."

Clara set a hand upon his arm, stalling him from following through on his threat. How dare the bastard say such a thing? Stephen wasn't sure if it stung more because there was a ring of truth to what he said or the fact that it was simply because Lord Peel had said it.

He did not need the prig before him telling him that he was not worthy of Lady Clara. He knew that himself. A boy born and raised in a cottage in Sandbach with three rooms, an impoverished aunt and very little means told him that himself. Not that he didn't think he was worthy of her hand, he would do as well as any other husband, but she was a duke's daughter, he was the son of servants who worked for nobility. He knew as well as anyone that she could never be his.

Stephen fisted his hands at his sides and Lord Peel cast a glance at his hands before bowing before Clara.

"I look forward to seeing you in town when you're there next, my lady. I wish you well."

Stephen watched him go, glad when the sound of the front door shutting echoed in the hall. "I apologize,

Clara. I have little patience with the man and he well knows it."

She turned, surprising him by taking him in her arms, linking her hands at his nape. "I like that you stood up to him. He's a bully and thinks he can get away with it. Not with you it would seem."

He stared down at her, marveling at her beauty. He reached down and slid his thumb across her jaw, so soft and perfect. "I have a confession."

She grinned, a devilish light entering her eyes. "You do. What is it?"

Stephen wrapped his arms about her waist, holding her close. "I want to kiss you."

She threw him a knowing smile and then leaned up and kissed him. Stephen met her halfway, having thought of little else from the moment he'd snuck out of her bed in the wee hours of yesterday morning.

"I have a confession too," she whispered against his lips.

"You do?" he asked, pausing. "What is it?"

Her fingers played with the hair at his nape, sending delicious shivers down his spine. "I've wanted to kiss you again too."

👑

*C*lara wasn't sure when she had fallen for Mr. Grant, but there was little doubt that her affections were truly engaged now. He'd supported her through one of the most difficult times in her life, never flinching or running away when days with her father had become too hard to bear. He'd been her rock, her support, the one person she could cry before and not feel shame. After taking him to her bed, there was no denying that she was falling in love with him.

She reached up again and kissed him. His lips were soft, willing, his tongue filling and inflaming her. His large hands clasped her hips, circling her back and pulling her hard against him. His previous kisses had been coaxing, teasing and soft in nature. She could not say the same about this one. Oh no, this one was demanding, hungry.

Starved.

His mouth covered hers, drawing her into a dance of desire and need. Clara squeaked and then chuckled when he swooped her into his arms, striding to a nearby leather chair and sitting down, placing her on his lap. She wiggled, making herself more comfortable as heat pooled at her core. He stared down at her a moment, their faces scant inches from each other and she reached up to clasp his stubbled jaw.

"What is it?" she asked, when he continued to consider her.

He shook his head, his lips remaining sealed.

She wrapped her arms about his neck, running his hair through her fingers. His locks were soft and thick. "Tell me," she pleaded, not wanting to have secrets between them.

"Only that," he said, pausing. "No matter how much time we have together, know that for me it will never be long enough."

Clara's heart ached at his words and although she did not know the full meaning behind them, she did wonder if he thought that their time would end. She certainly did not wish it to end anytime soon, there were so many more things she wanted to do, to experience with him. But that did not mean that Stephen had different plans for his future, different goals and dreams other than a wife.

She started at her own thought of becoming his wife. A duke's daughter, she'd not given much thought at all that this, whatever it was between her and Stephen, would lead anywhere.

She had been so against him in the past, cutting and dismissive. Shame washed over her that she'd been so awful and judgmental. Her friends would certainly be shocked at her turned-about opinion, and there would be some who would distance themselves from her over her choice.

His lips brushed her neck and all thoughts of her friends and their prejudices toward those who had less than them flew out of her mind. His hand moved up to cup her breast, which felt tight and enlarged under her gown. His finger and thumb found her pebbled nipple and he rolled it between his fingers. She gasped through the kiss, wanting him with a feverish need.

The kiss turned inflammatory as she explored his body. His chest was hard, his breathing as rapid as hers and she could feel beneath her palm the hard ridges of muscle that lined his stomach. There were too many clothes, too much separating them. All she wanted was to be rid of their clothing so she may see all of him again.

"Touch me." His voice was husky and low and she could hear the need that tremored through his words.

Clara stroked lower and the pit of her stomach clenched when her hand closed around his manhood. Thick and hard and ready for her.

"Clara," he gasped when she stroked him. "Stop," he said, his hand halting hers. "Or you'll find I'll lose myself in my breeches like a green lad."

"I don't mind doing this for you." She met his gaze and without looking away, flicked open each of the buttons holding his breeches closed. A muscle ticked in his jaw, his face took on a hard edge and she marveled at how handsome he was.

She glanced down to see his member as it sprung free from his breeches. Perfect, just as she remembered. Veins ran the length of his manhood, and a little droplet of moisture sat at the head of his phallus. Clara wiped it away with her thumb.

He groaned, laying his head back against the seat.

"You undo me."

His words pushed her on and she wrapped her hand about him, stroking him, playing and teasing his flesh. Marveling as it swelled and deepened to a purple hue.

He wrenched her in for a kiss, her mouth opening for him as he devoured her. Moisture pooled between her legs as he moaned through their kiss and that's when she felt him push up into her hold, pumping against her hand as he found his pleasure.

Clara broke the kiss, her body aching for what she now knew he could give her.

"Now it's my turn," he said, his gaze heavy with determination and heat. Clara shivered, expectation thrumming through her at being with him again.

"What would you like me to do?"

*W*hat would he like her to do? What wouldn't he like her to do would be a better question. She'd brought him pleasure and now he was going to make her shatter in his arms. He hoisted her to straddle his legs, fighting with her black gown to pool at her waist. There was too much clothing, too much separating them and he wanted it gone.

She lowered onto his lap and he reached beneath her gown, sliding his hand up her silky-soft thigh until he reached the apex between her legs. He slid his hand across her mons, delicious moisture met his fingers. She was ready for him, and his cock twitched at the idea of sheathing himself in her hot heat.

"I'm going to touch you now," he whispered against her

neck, breathing deep her scent of jasmine. She smelled good enough to eat and the idea of doing just that, tasting her, kissing her to climax almost had him picking her up, laying her on the settee and delving between her legs.

She nodded, her cheeks flushed. He slid his hand over her flesh, cupping her. Her hands spiked into his hair, pulling his strands. Her body undulated above him as he found the slit in her pantalets and rubbed her sweet nubbin in a circular motion.

A breathy moan escaped from her lips as she continued to slide against his hand. Stephen slipped one finger into her hot core. She gasped, her hands frantically clasping his shoulders for purpose. The sight of her coming undone by his touch left him growing hard at a rapid pace.

"Do you want more, my lady?" he asked, reaching up and hooking his hand along the bodice of her gown. He slid the material over her ample bosom, exposing her to him. Stephen could not look away from the sight she made. That of a woman who was enjoying his touch, a woman learning of what pleasures can be had between a man and woman.

He leaned forward, kissing her puckered nipple before taking it into his mouth. Her fingers dug into his skin.

"Oh yes," she gasped, rocking against him. "Please."

Stephen took his hand away, reaching around to clasp one perfect buttock and hoisting her against his manhood. Her heat slid against his cock, wet and ready. Her eyes widened at the newfound sensation and damn it all to hell it felt good. Too good not to have again. Too good to walk away from.

He guided her to slide against his cock. "We can do this without going any further."

She nodded, her eyes glazed with desire and he grinned. He took her nipple into his mouth, scraping the puckered flesh with his teeth before laving it with his tongue.

Clara pushed her sex against his. He was rock hard and if she did not find her release soon he'd come again.

"Stephen," she gasped, her hips rocking and pushing against him with increasing tempo.

He held her steady, his balls hard and aching. "Come for me, darling," he said, pushing up against her as he pulled her onto him from behind.

She threw her head back, gasping as her body shattered in his arms. "Oh yes, Stephen," she cried. There was no use trying to stop, he climaxed again. Her breasts bounced before him and he reached up, pinching her nipple as she rode him through her pleasure.

Clara collapsed to his side, and he wrapped her up in his arms, loving the fact she fit him so well.

"Well, that was certainly pleasurable," she said, grinning up at him. "However will we stop such interludes?" He clasped her cheek, kissing her slowly.

"Yes, it was," he said when at last he pulled away. "And there are other things we can do besides that will be just as pleasurable if you're interested."

Her eyes brightened with interest and he inwardly chuckled. "Really? However will I keep away from you?"

He grinned. "That, my lady, is why you will not."

hree days later Clara received a note from her friend Lady Davenport from London regarding an article that had been published in the paper. Julia had sent her a clipping of the piece and Clara slumped onto the sofa in the upstairs parlor as she read words that hundreds of peers too would have devoured.

A little image had been drawn for the amusement of the paper's readership depicting a woman, similar in coloring to her and a man of similar features to Mr. Grant in a compromising position in a library. The article mentioned a daughter of a duke having been seduced by one not of her rank and implied that her stay in the country was solely due to being ruined by the fiend not worth her notice.

She rubbed her brow, pain spiking behind her eyes and for a moment the room spun. Who had written such a piece of malicious text and why? Clara read it again, certain that she could not be mistaken and again the words jumped out at her, taunting, laughing and ruining her.

The little drawing had the woman dressed in black and there was no doubt in her mind that it was her that the article had been written about. And there had been only one other person who had seen her standing beside Mr. Grant in a library in such a way.

Lord Peel.

The urge to scrunch up the article in her hand grew the more she thought about the man who had tried to take liberties that were not freely given, and now this. To disgrace her in such a way when she had never done anything to him, other than rebuff his advances was not to be borne. Had her father been alive she was certain that he would never have been so disrespectful to her.

A duke's daughter.

Clara blinked back the tears and she stood, walking to the window to look over the grounds. Is this what society would do to her now that her father was gone? Or was this simply a taunt, a warning that she should remove Mr. Grant from her life or suffer worse embarrassments?

Something told her it was the latter.

The sound of footsteps sounded in the hall outside and she quickly wiped at her cheeks, turning to face the door and whoever had called. Although she already had an inkling of who it would be.

A footman knocked on the door, stepping inside and announcing Mr. Grant. She bade him enter, not moving from the window lest he see her upset.

"Mr. Grant, how good of you to call." Clara clasped her hands at her front, unsure of how to tell him what had been disclosed to her today. He would be furious she imagined and hurt, but would he see the implications for them at this affront?

The footman closed the door, leaving them alone and Stephen smiled, coming over to her and pulling her into his arms. She went willingly, breathing deep his scent of sandalwood and goodness. For he was a good man, no matter what she'd once thought of him. How wrong she'd been all those years ago, and what she was about to say to him would be very hard for them both to hear.

"Clara," he said, kissing her soundly.

She lost herself a moment in the embrace, not wanting to face the truth of their situation. Wanting to for a little while longer be cocooned in their bubble in Kent.

"I missed you."

"I only saw you yesterday," she said, trying to make light of his words and yet, they rang as true to her as they did to him. She'd missed him also. In fact, she'd come to realize of late with growing concern that she hated when he left.

"Come sit with me, Stephen. There is something you need to see."

A small frown played upon his brow, but he followed her to the sofa and sat beside her. Clara picked up the article from the small table where they sat and handed it to him. He read it quickly, his mouth turning down in disapproval, a deep scowl between his eyes.

"How dare the bastard? I ought to call him out."

She met his eyes, reading the truth behind his words. "I thought the same. This is most certainly the work of Lord Peel."

Stephen screwed the clipping up and threw it into the fire. "Do not react or show any concern over such an insulting piece. When he knows that we will not respond there will be little he can do."

Except start to make up stories to suit his nefarious means. Ruin her reputation forever...

Clara clasped her hands in her lap to stop their shaking. "You know Lord Peel. He's vindictive and doesn't like to not get his own way. My disinterest in his attempts of courtship have brought this on, and that you're the one gentleman whom he never thought to have to consider as a possible rival has led him to act out in such a way."

He grinned, taking her hand, his thumb running circles atop it. "Am I a rival for your hand, Lady Clara?"

Her gaze met his. Never before had they talked of courtship, that what they had been doing with each other these past weeks would ever lead to anything more lasting. Did Mr. Grant wish for there to be more between them, and if he did, did Clara want there to be?

"I had not thought about it." The lie almost choked her and she cleared her throat as Stephen narrowed his eyes on her. "A stolen kiss here and there is not marriage inducing, is it not?"

He pulled back a little, watching her warily. "I think what we've been doing is a little more than kissing, my lady." He studied her a moment before he said, "I will be honest and tell you that at first I did not think of such a possibility at all. You're far above me in rank and wealth and there is little that will change my circumstances. I do not need a London lord to write an article and draw a picture to tell me that truth.

"But I've come to care for you, more than I thought would ever be possible knowing our tumultuous history. I would be a liar if I did not admit that I've thought of you as my wife. As quickly as I thought such a thing I dismissed it due to our different circumstances. It does not mean, however, that I do not want such a future with you."

Clara pulled her hand away, rising and going to stand before the fire. She bit the inside of her bottom lip, not sure how she would get through this conversation that they had to have. A conversation long overdue.

"I do care for you, Stephen. So very much," she said, meeting his gaze. "But I cannot marry you. There is too much of a divide between us and this article is just the first of many such articles that will nail home what the *ton* would think of my marriage to you. We will be ridiculed, shunned, our children too no doubt. People will laugh at how changeable I am. They all know that I once despised you, and now look at me. I…" She stopped speaking, shocked that she was about to say a word she'd never uttered to anyone else ever in her life.

Stephen's face shuttered, all warmth seeping from his blue-green orbs. "All this time I thought that you had changed and yet you're still the same. A woman afraid of what others think of you. Do not forget who you are, Lady Clara. You're a duke's daughter, an heiress, no one can touch you if you do not let them."

She shook her head, wanting to believe his words but knowing she could not. She was not that strong. She may have seemed to everyone that she was formidable, cold and above reproach, but she was not. "Whether I like it or not, they're my friends. For the rest of my life I will have to attend the Season and be a part of that world. I cannot be ostracized. I have no one, Stephen. No family, nothing left to me that is blood. My friends are all whom I have left."

"You have me. Am I not enough?"

Oh, he was enough, he'd always be enough, but it could not just be the two of them forever.

"I cannot just have you, Stephen. There are other things to consider and you know that."

He stood and ran a hand through his hair. He strode toward the door and fear shot through her that he'd leave. "If you loved me I would be more than enough, Clara. You're certainly enough for me. You're all that I want in this world. I live to hear your voice each day, to kiss your lips, and breathe in your scent. I did not think I was alone in this emotion."

She took a step toward him and stopped when he held up a hand to halt her. "You are not alone in that, but I cannot marry you. My marriage should be the joining of two great families. For all that you are, your beautiful soul and heart, I cannot give you mine in return. I'm sorry."

"Spineless and cold to the very end. Had I not known you these past weeks I would not have thought it possible for someone to be so callous." He laughed, the sound mocking. "You do not disappoint, Lady Clara. A viper to the very end."

"Stephen," she pleaded, striding toward him. She grabbed his arm as he went to leave and he shrugged off her hold.

"What, my lady? What is there left to say?"

Her heart shattered at the broken look in his eyes. She'd made him feel that way. She had been the one to do this to him and she hated herself for it. "You're right, I am scared of what others will think, what they will do to me. Lord Peel's threat is there for all to see and next Season when I'm in town his little article may see me ostracized already. That world is all I have left. Please understand, I have no one left to protect me from them."

His face contorted into a look of contempt. "Nonsense. You have me, at least, you had me," he corrected. He turned for the door and wrenched it open. "Have a happy life with your lord, Lady Clara. May the nobility and all its trappings bring you joy."

She stared after him, his words echoing through her mind like a death knell. She swallowed the sob that wanted to wrench from her. Had they just parted? Parted forever? Her stomach roiled and she stumbled to the door in her haste to catch up to him. She jerked the door open only to see no sight of him.

Clara ran for the back of the house, ignoring the startled gasps and looks her staff gave her. She pushed open the servants' door that was a mere few short steps to the stables only to see Stephen pushing his horse out of the yard and toward his own estate at a full gallop.

"Stephen," she yelled, heedless of who heard her. "Stephen, wait!" *I've made a mistake...*

She watched until she could no longer see him and jumped when a clap of thunder sounded overhead. Clara looked up at the sky, watching as the first drops of heavy, large raindrops fell from the sky.

"Damn it," she muttered, turning for the indoors. She would travel over to his estate tomorrow and make it right. Once they had both calmed down and she was thinking more clearly, she would amend this riff. It was not over between them. Not yet at least.

CHAPTER 12

Scotland, Mid-March 1810

"That's it, I've had it with you, Brother. Eat your breakfast, bathe and get on your horse back to England. You cannot mope about Scotland for the rest of your life."

"I can and I will," Stephen replied, moving about the one piece of bacon he had on his plate. He stared down at the food, knowing he was moping and that his sister was right. He really did need to return to his estate that he'd promised his brother-in-law he'd take care of for him. But how could he return there, the one place he knew she would be.

Clara.

He clenched his jaw, reaching for his cup of coffee. The thought of her always brought both longing and anger in equal measures. He'd not seen her since the day of their parting, almost four months ago now. He'd packed up his belongings that very day, placed his steward in charge of Ashby Cottage and rode for Scotland. Multiple times he'd thought to turn around, go back and fight for her. Make her see that he was more than what he'd been born, a common man with very little to recommend him other than his loyalty and good character. He was the man for her. If only the stubborn wench would see it.

Instead, she'd thrown him off. Told him to his face that he was not good enough for her exalted breeding.

He shook his head, throwing his napkin down beside him and pushing back his chair. "I'll see you at luncheon."

"No you won't," his sister said, standing and reaching the door before he had a chance to escape. "I've instructed a servant to pack up your things and at this very moment they are being bundled into a carriage. You're returning to England today and that is the end of it."

Stephen glared at his twin, turning to her husband who sat at the head of the table, watching them both with amusement. "Dinna look at me, lad. I'll not be going against my wife. I suggest ye shouldna go against yer sister either."

"You're kicking me out?"

His sister's shoulders slumped and she clasped his hands. Hers were warm and soft and it made him miss feeling such a way as well. He'd been cold since he'd left England, although he wasn't sure if it was because of the climate in the Highlands or because his heart had simply stopped beating.

"We would never use such terms, but we are setting you on a correct path. That being south and to London. You need to speak to Lady Clara. Maybe she has changed her mind. Your absence may have been the catalyst that had made her see that you were indeed the man she loved and wanted as her husband. Not some stodgy, old titled lord."

Laird Mackintosh cleared his throat. "I hope that isna a reflection on what ye thought of me, my love."

His sister turned and the adoration that was etched on her face whenever she glanced at her husband made Stephen want to both retch and cry. He was a foolish fop.

"You're Scottish. I'm referring to the English only, my dear."

The laird chuckled and cut into his kippers. Stephen sighed. "She's probably betrothed by now. She had many suitors besides myself before her father died. Louise wrote in her last letter that Clara was back in town and taking part in the Season. What's left of it in any case."

"You know that I've never been fond of Lady Clara. Heavens, she was not the nicest to us, but if she was different with you, redeemed herself and you fell in love with that side of her, then you need to go win her back. Do not live to regret doing nothing, Brother. That is not who we are. We're Grants. We get what we want."

"'Tis true, I can vouch for that," the laird said, agreeing with his wife.

Stephen stopped himself from rolling his eyes. "I will go and I will see what is at play in London, but I cannot promise that anything will come of it between us. I've not heard from her, and nor have I written in turn. It is possible that it is too late."

"It is never too late to win back one's love. I can vouch for that." Sophie clasped his arm, walking him to the door in the great hall in which they ate most of their meals here in Scotland. "Go, my dearest brother. I expect to hear news soon of your impending marriage."

He threw her a small smile, not wanting to ruin her hope that he himself was feeling very little of. Even so, he would return to town and see what was afoot, and if Clara was as indifferent to him as her words of dismissal made her out to be four months past.

CHAPTER 13

London, April 1810

Clara stood in the ballroom of Lord and Lady Davenport's home and only just stopped herself from gasping out loud. Tonight was the first time she'd seen Mr. Grant in some time, and for the first hour of the assembly, she'd not been able to look away from the striking appearance he cut within the nobility.

His superfine coat and silk breeches were cut to fit him perfectly, his silver waistcoat and faultlessly tied cravat accentuated his lovely jaw and sinful mouth. She'd not been able to look away, and not only because he made her body yearn with a longing she'd pushed down over their time apart. But because her friend, a woman whom she had at times vented her dislike of Stephen was currently hanging on his every word across the room from her.

Clara took a sip of her ratafia as she stood with a group of friends, all married and all thoroughly engrossed in their conversations regarding marriage and children. Clara had tried to take part as much as she could, listen and impart any advice that she could, but since Clara was unmarried and not a mother, her friends were often dismissive of her input and so she'd learned to stay quiet and simply nod when they looked her way.

It was easier than to tell them their conversations were boring and if she were not their friend she would have fallen asleep on the spot hours ago.

"Is that not your neighbor, Clara?" Julia said, staring in the direction that she'd last seen Stephen. "I did not know Lord Davenport had invited him."

Clara feigned surprise and glanced about until she spotted the dratted man. Oh yes, it was him, laughing and talking as if she did not exist. And she supposed she did not any longer. Not since she had told him he was not worth her time simply because he was not born nobility.

What a horrible person she was.

"Yes, I believe so," she said, matter-of-fact. "He must be back from Scotland."

"Visiting that dreadful sister of his, I assume. Remember, Clara what fun we had during Lady Graham's first Season?" Julia turned to the women about them. "We did not like them you see. Mr. Grant was quite rude and cutting toward Lady Clara and so we ensured we never went out of our way to befriend her or make her welcome. We succeeded too."

"Except Miss Grant became the Marchioness Graham. So I suppose we did not in truth," Clara said, wanting to remind Julia that Miss Grant had become a marchioness while she had only married an earl. As for Clara she had not married anyone.

Clara looked down at her gown of blue muslin with a silk underlay. It was so very fine and pretty, and she'd made the extra effort tonight knowing Stephen would be in attendance. All day her stomach had fluttered at the thought of seeing him again. He did not disappoint. He was as handsome as she remembered and after all they had suffered through together, she wanted to go up to him and speak to him again. She wanted to know how he was. Was he happy? Did he miss her as much as she missed him?

She swallowed the lump in her throat. She was not happy. Had not been so for a very long time and could not remember the last time she laughed. Certainly it would've been back when they were at Chidding Hall together.

"Why Mr. Grant is back in London is anyone's guess. It's not like he has a fortune. He's a son of nobody knows who. Surely he does not think to make an advantageous marriage within our sphere."

Clara cast a glance his way and from the way women of her acquaintance were lapping up his every word she concurred that Lady Davenport was wrong about that. He would make an advantageous marriage, especially for a woman of wealth who wanted the connection of nobility. Mr. Grant was, after all, the brother-in-law to one of the most influential marquesses in England and one of the wealthiest.

"You're wrong, Julia. Mr. Grant I should imagine will marry well and soon if his popularity is any indication. Do not be so judgmental. If you keep scowling, those lines between your brows will become permanent."

Julia gasped and yet her eyes were as cold as ice. "Clara, how could you say such a thing to me? I thought we were friends."

Clara shrugged, taking in all the sets of wide-eyed women staring at her after her words. None of them did she care about. Certainly, she did not care what their opinion of her would be, or if they would include her in forthcoming events should she follow her heart. Only one person did she care for and she'd thrown him away as if he were worthless, when in truth, this world she occupied, the fickle and fake friendships she'd made over the years, those were what was really worthless.

Not the genuine man who had aided, supported and loved her all of those weeks in Kent.

He did love her. That she was sure about more than anything else in the world, but did he love her still? He'd never said the words, but they were there, every day he showed his affection by being her pillar of strength, her support, in every touch and look, not to mention his wicked kisses.

"We are friends, Julia, but I find that my behavior over the last few years toward Mr. Grant and his family was shameful. He's a good man, just as his sisters did not deserve our slights and wicked remarks. We, all of us, owe them an apology. We should not like to be treated in such a way."

"No one would dare treat us in that way," Julia said, smirking as if Clara were making a joke.

"Not to your face at least," Clara said, dipping into a curtsy and leaving. She ignored the startled gasps from her friends, and sought out Lady Graham. She owed her an apology first and foremost and then she would find Stephen and remove him from the ladies who thought to win his affections. They were not his to give to anyone else for they were hers and hers alone.

Clara found Lady Graham standing beside her husband, the woman's eyes clouding in unease as Clara came up to them. She dipped into a curtsy, smiling a little to try to put the woman at ease. How awful of her to have treated her ladyship so appallingly simply because she had once harbored hopes toward the Marquess being her husband.

"Good evening, Lady Graham. My lord," she said, coming to stand beside her.

Her ladyship threw her husband a look of bewilderment before smiling at Clara. The gesture did not reach her ladyship's eyes and Clara sighed, hoping she could make things right between them. No matter what had happened between her and Stephen, she did want her feud with Lady Graham to come to an end.

"Good evening, Lady Clara. It is good to see you back in town."

Clara nodded, glancing back out toward where she'd left her friends. Most if not all of them had noted her location and many were watching with rapt attention. No doubt they expected Clara to be her usual, cutting self.

Clara turned to face her ladyship. "This may seem a little strange, and out of nowhere, but I wanted to apologize to both you and the Marquess. I have been abominably rude in the past, cutting and frankly a trial to be around, and neither of you deserved my atrocious behavior. This is quite forward of me I know to be so outspoken, but for whatever it is worth, I am sorry for my actions in the past and I want you both to know that it will never happen again." Clara glanced back to where she'd seen Stephen last and she shivered at seeing him watching her, his dark, contemplative gaze fixed on her person.

Lady Graham reached out and clasped her hand, squeezing it a little. "Thank you, Lady Clara for your apology. It is most readily accepted and I do hope we're able from this night on to be friends."

Clara turned back and smiled at her ladyship, pleasure coursing through her at her ladyship's words. "I would like that too, my lady. Very much."

*

Stephen watched to see his sister's reaction to Clara coming over to speak to her, but from the delight and animated conversation they were now having after a stifled start, they looked for all the world to see as if they were old, reunited friends.

He narrowed his eyes, wondering at it. Inane chatter floated about him regarding the weather, gossip and the latest betrothals to be announced about London from his shadow for the evening, Miss Huxtable. He couldn't understand why she had taken a liking to him all of a sudden or why she and her gaggle of friends found his conversation so very interesting.

Stephen stifled a sigh, wanting to escape and yet not knowing how he could without causing offense.

"Do you not agree, Mr. Grant?"

His gaze shot to the women about him, each of their gazes set on him as if he was about to impart some grand advice they could not live without. "I do apologize, what was the question?" He shook himself out of being distracted by the woman who bothered him to no end and concentrated on the conversation at hand.

"We were discussing the merits of marriage. That a woman of wealth marrying a gentleman of little means is looked upon more favorably than a man of wealth marrying a woman of little wealth or connections. Do you not agree?"

Stephen swallowed, well aware that each of the women who stood before him were heiresses, but with fathers who were lower ranked on the nobility ladder. He supposed his connection to the Marquess Graham, one of the richest lords in England had something to do with his newfound popularity.

Not to mention he'd heard whispers about town that his association with the Duke of Law's daughter had been noted.

"I must admit that I have not given the notion much thought, but I think that if a couple were to marry, I would hope that they cared for, if not loved, each other. I dislike the idea that wealth or connections would sway the union." Such as it had with Clara and him. He clamped his mouth shut lest he say anything else. The women before him did not know what had transpired between him and Clara, nor did they know their conversation grazed very close to his own truth.

That his love had been thrown back in his face simply because he was not titled. That Clara was worried what society would say about her marriage to him.

He knew what they would say. That he'd married her for her money and that she had married beneath her status. That his family had carried on their coup of marrying titled rich people of the *beau monde*.

Little did it matter that his sisters adored and loved their husbands and long saw past their husbands' titles to the men who were beneath all that finery. Stephen had seen past Clara and the decoration piece she was when in town to the woman beneath. The one who had a heart, cared deeply and loved passionately.

Now that he was back in London he wasn't sure if there was any future between them. Tonight was the first time he'd seen her in four months and the sight of her almost brought him to his knees. Her gown of blue muslin draped over her body like a second skin. Her lithe figure and creamy white skin were as perfect as he remembered and he ached to take her in his arms, to pull her close and kiss the little freckle that sat directly beneath her ear.

He wanted her, but he wanted her to want him too. Love him for who he was, even if that was someone who was not of her stature.

He sipped from his glass of wine when the Earl Darwin bowed before her, asking for her hand in a dance. He gritted his teeth, finishing the drink instead of storming into the middle of the ballroom and ripping her from his lordship's arms.

Stephen inwardly groaned when the first strains of a

waltz commenced and Clara smiled as his lordship pulled her into his arms. For a moment his gaze fixated on the bastard's hand as it held her waist before he bowed to the women about him. "If you'll excuse me." He strode from the room, heading toward the terrace doors. Anywhere but where he could see Clara smiling and enjoying herself in another's arms. A man's arms whom she deemed worthy of her rank. A man who by fortune of birth was an earl.

"Mr. Grant. Are you well? You left us so suddenly."

He let go of the balustrade he was leaning on. Damn it, he cringed at the sound of Miss Huxtable's voice behind him. Why the devil had she followed him? He looked up the terrace and spotted only one other couple. Relief poured through him that they were at least not alone.

"I'm very well, thank you. The room is simply a little warm."

Her gaze flicked over him in an assessing manner and he raised his brow at her candor. "You should return inside, Miss Huxtable before you're missed."

She sauntered up to him and he glanced back to where the other couple had been only to see that they had disappeared. He took a step back, his legs hitting the stone balustrade and halting his escape.

"Mama will not miss me." She grinned and he inwardly cursed. "Will you waltz out here with me?"

"Miss Huxtable, go back inside at once before you ruin yourself."

Stephen's gaze whipped to the doors and to where Lady Clara stood, a disapproving frown on her normally pretty visage.

"My lady," Miss Huxtable said, dipping into a curtsy and scuttling back inside as if the devil himself was nipping at her silk slippers.

Stephen leaned back against the railing, crossing his

arms. "Lady Clara. It's been a long time." Too damn long. He took in every delicious morsel that was Clara, soaking her up after months of not seeing her, hearing her voice. He'd missed her more than he'd thought he would. Stephen had told himself it was for the best that they parted when they did. Before too many emotions became involved. Before anyone lost their heart. But seeing her standing before him, a look of disapproval on her face, well, it only hammered home how much he'd been fooling himself.

No matter what she thought or the words spoken on his lack of breeding, he was in love with her. Had been in love with her for quite some time if he were honest with himself.

She stepped out onto the flagstones, coming to stand before him. "What do you think you're doing out here with Miss Huxtable? If her father caught you in such a position, he'd have you married within the week."

He shrugged. "Miss Huxtable is a sweet girl. I'm sure marriage to her would not be a trial." The narrowing of Clara's eyes brought forth a wave of pleasure. He wanted her to be annoyed. Wanted her to see what she'd lost.

Him...

CHAPTER 14

*C*lara fought not to scratch Stephen's eyes out over his blind stupidity. Did he not realize that if he compromised a debutante he'd be forced to marry her? Clara pushed away the knowledge that she only cared about such things because if Stephen married someone else it would mean he could not marry her.

She sighed, hating that she'd pushed him away. That she'd hurt him with a truth that held no sway on her anymore. Having been back in society these past weeks had proven to her that she no longer cared what her friends thought of those ranked lower than them. Those with more or less funds at their disposal.

Walking out onto the terrace this evening and seeing Stephen with another woman… Now that she did care about. It had taken all her years of learning to behave like a lady should to stop her from grabbing Miss Huxtable by her curls and hurling her back inside with an almighty push.

"Miss Huxtable is not for you."

He scoffed, shaking his head. "Let me guess as to why, my lady. Because I'm not rich enough to satisfy her father? Some people, you forget, do not let such facts influence their choice."

"I suppose you mean that I allow such prejudices to influence my choices." She moved along the terrace and heard him follow her. "I suppose I have allowed such opinions to do so, but it was only because of the circumstances of my birth and my upbringing that guided me into that way of thinking."

"Does not change the fact that yet again you've stepped into my life and halted what could possibly be a future for me. Miss Huxtable is a delightful girl and who didn't seem to be inclined to care about my lowly birth. Perhaps it would be best if you returned inside and had Miss Huxtable join me again on the terrace."

Clara unfisted her hands at her sides, and fought to calm her heart. How dare he threaten her with such actions? She ought to call his bluff and return to the ballroom and do exactly what he'd asked. She cast a glance at him at her side, his hands clasped behind his back as they strolled along a darkened portion of the terrace. "How changeable men are. One moment you were courting me and here you are, at a ball in London and attempting to court others if my observations of you this evening are correct."

Stephen barked out a laugh, the sound condescending. "That opinion could be said of you as well, my lady. Four months past you were in my arms, all heat and passion, and here you are doing the same as I, since I'm not worthy of your hand."

Clara glared at him. "I ought to marry a lord, someone rich and titled, heaven knows plenty have been trying to court me." All true, since her return to town, her multiple estates and money had been a beacon of light for those who would court such wealth. All of the gentlemen had paled in comparison to the one who stood beside her. How she had fallen for the man who had vexed, challenged and rudely rebuffed her at times astounded her still, but she had and now no one else would do for her.

She wanted him.

Not that she was willing to spout such truths. The sight of him with Miss Huxtable had halted that notion. For the moment at least.

"Such an outcome would certainly make your friends happy."

Clara took a step back as he advanced on her. His eyes bored into her and left her steps unsteady. He looked so angry and annoyed and God help her, she was glad of it. Glad he was showing some emotion after all this time apart. She had thought him completely lost and indifferent only today after four months of not seeing him. His reactions to her words certainly gave rise to hope.

A hope that after what she'd said to him, she did not deserve to have.

"It would. It would make them extremely happy," she taunted.

Another step forward. Another step back. Clara slipped around him and started for the corner of the house. They did not need to be seen arguing and she had little doubt that was exactly what they were about to do. If not worse than they already were.

This side of the house they only had the moonlight to guide their way and Clara stood at the terrace balustrade, looking over the shadowy gardens beyond.

"Do you mean that?" he asked, his words low and tremulous behind her.

She shut her eyes, knowing it was the time for truth. "No. I do not."

*S*tephen leaned forward, unsure he'd heard Clara right. No? Did that mean... He turned her to face him, her beauty catching him by surprise for a moment before he steeled himself to find out the truth. "What does that mean?"

He didn't let her go. Couldn't if he were honest. He'd wanted to touch her for months now, to hear her voice, to be with her as they had been in Kent. His hands slid down her arms, the softness of her skin as smooth as the silk gloves she wore.

She glanced up at him and he read the longing in her eyes and he wanted to comfort her. To tell her the truth about their time apart, but he could not. Not yet.

"I was wrong, Stephen. So very wrong, and now I fear it is too late."

"No." It was never too late. Not for what he hoped she was about to say. "Tell me, Clara. Tell me what you're thinking." Or he would expire if she did not.

"Our parting has been one of the loneliest times I've ever endured. After you left I threw myself into looking after my estates, the staff and farms, but I could not get you out of my mind. I realized I made a mistake in sending you away. In fact, I came after you the day you left, but you could not hear me calling. And now tonight, seeing the many women fawn at your feet, well, I knew I had to tell the truth before it was too late."

He bit back a grin at her words, not quite believing what she was saying. "And that was?" he asked.

"I was wrong how I spoke to you all those months ago in Kent. After what Lord Peel wrote about us I was frightened I'd be ruined and my prospects along with it. But then being back in town I realized that I held more power than I gave myself credit for. Daughter to the late Duke of Law and all that position entails makes me immune to a lot of Lord Peel's nastiness. People know my character, and they will not believe his lordship's words. While some of my friends may slight me in society over my choice of husband, those who do are not the ones worthy of my friendship."

He closed the space between them, took her face in his hands and kissed her. She fell into his arms, holding him close and he deepened the kiss, having missed her so terribly. "I made a mistake too," he said between kisses, pushing her back toward the side of the house and away from prying eyes should anyone walk about the corner.

"You did?"

"I did," he said, kissing her again. "I should never have left you. I should have stayed and fought for you. Made you see what you had to come to realize on your own."

She clasped his jaw, scratching at the little growth of stubble that sat on his face. "And what was that? Remind me."

"That we're meant for each other. Even when we disagree we're perfect for each other."

He pulled back, kneeling before her. Clara's eyes widened and she bit her lip.

"You're the love of my life, Lady Clara. Marry me?" he asked, trepidation seeping into his blood even with the knowledge of what she'd said. Still the fear persisted that she would choose someone more equal to her.

She pulled him up to stand, leaping into his arms. He held her close, breathing in the delicious smell of jasmine and the wonderful future that was within his view. "I will marry you, Mr. Grant." She pulled back a little, her eyes bright with unshed tears. "I adore and love you too, even if you drive me to distraction most of the time."

He chuckled, lifting her off her feet and spinning her. "You bother me too, my lady, but promise me one thing."

Clara nodded. "Anything," she said, watching him.

"Don't ever stop being you."

She smiled and his heart thumped hard in his chest. He kissed her again, deep and long and with each brush of her lips across his, the fears he'd harbored slipped away and gave way to the possibility of them. The future was grand and he'd ensure always happy. For them both.

Always…

EPILOGUE

*C*lara sat on the river back at Chidding Hall, her son stood beside Stephen, both with fishing rods in their hands as they tried to catch their dinner. She smiled as the two most precious people in her world spoke of the fish breeds available in Kent and what sizes they may catch if they were lucky.

"Did grandfather really not allow anyone to fish here?" their son, Maximus asked, looking over his shoulder at her.

Clara nodded, smiling at the many days her father had ranted and argued the point as to why no one should fish in this very stream, unless it was their gamekeepers of course. "Until your father that is. I probably should have realized at that point that your father was the one for me since father approved him."

Stephen threw her a knowing smile before turning back to look at the river.

"I wish I had known Grandfather, Mama."

She swallowed the lump that rose in her throat that always happened when they spoke of her dearest father and all the wonderful things he'd missed. "He was the best of men, Max. And he would have loved to have met you as well. I know he would be proud of the young man you've become."

They were all proud. Max had excelled at Eton and would go on to college when the time came. Their only child, she would miss him dearly when he left, but, she reminded herself, there were still some years to go before that happened, he was only thirteen after all.

Stephen placed his fishing rod down and started toward her, coming to sit at her side. He leaned over and kissed her softly, and her stomach fluttered as it always had from the first time she'd argued with him in Hyde Park to the day they had promised their lives to each other before God.

"What are you writing in that journal of yours?" He tried to take it from her and she snatched it away, holding it away from him.

"Nothing that concerns you," she teased. In truth, it concerned him and their little family in all ways. All their memories were in her journals, their lives, their travels, heartbreaks and triumphs. Everything written down so she would never forget, even if she one day succumbed to the illness that took her father. Not that she had any fears that her mind was failing her, but even so, at least she would never forget her life.

"Maybe one day you will let me read them."

Clara put down her journal and shuffled closer to Stephen, wrapping her arms about his waist. He pulled her close, his hand idly running up and down her spine, sending a delicious shiver through her person.

"One day I will, but not this day." She grinned up at him.

He reached around and slipped a strand of her hair that had tumbled free of its pin behind her ear. "You're as beautiful as the day we met. I adore you."

Heat rose on her cheeks and she marveled that he could still make her blush after all these years. "I love you too."

Their son made a gagging sound and she laughed, knowing he disliked that they were so public with their affection. And they had been from the moment they were married, whether in town during the Season or at one of their many estates, they did not shy away from showing their love for each another.

Lord Peel had tried to mar Clara's character, but Stephen and her Scottish brother-in-law, Laird Mackintosh, had put paid to his lordship's continual threats by a good one of their own one day at Whites when no one had been about.

She grinned at the memory of it. Her fears that society would shun her for marrying a man beneath her social status had too been unfounded and instead of turning their noses up at them, they had never said a word. Certainly not to their faces at least, and she was content with that. Invitations arrived by the dozen each day as if she'd married a duke in lieu of a Mister.

How silly she'd been to have almost thrown away the one man who had made her life worth living. Had given her the gift of their boy, who squealed, reeling in his line all of a sudden.

Clara jumped and Stephen ran over to Max, helping him hold the rod as they reeled in the fish.

"I've caught one! It's a big one I think," Max said through his exertions.

She went over to them, watching as a large trout landed on the bank, gasping for air. Stephen patted Max's back, congratulating him.

"Well done, Max. I don't believe I've seen such a large fish being caught here for some years," she said.

"Not even father has caught one so big?" Max asked, his eyes bright and excited.

"Well, I'm sure I have," Stephen interjected. Clara shook her head.

"Not even your father." She took the rod from Max as he picked up the fish, holding it at his side.

"Mrs. Pennell is going to be well pleased with this fish. Pity you did not catch one as well today, Father."

Stephen messed up Max's hair before their son turned for the house, trying to run as fast as he could, the large fish in his hand an impediment to his speed. Stephen reached over, taking the rod from her and taking her hand.

"I'm sure I've caught a fish of that size. You're mistaken, my lady."

"Hmm," she said, "If you have it was before you gained approval to fish here from my father and I never saw it."

He shot a look at her, his eyes wide. "I never fished here before I was allowed and you well know it. I wouldn't dare bring the wrath of the Lady Clara Quinton upon my head."

She chuckled. "To think that you and I officially started in this very spot. I can still see you walking across the grounds with Father, asking him if you may fish in his river. I was so annoyed that you had dared come here, but then I was pleased too. I always enjoyed sparring with you. A little at least."

He pulled her to a stop, throwing the rod to the ground and hoisting her up against him. Her heart thrummed loudly in her ears and she reached up, clasping his face in her hands. How lucky she was he was hers. "I always enjoyed verbally sparring with you also, and everything else." He grinned.

Stephen leaned down and kissed her and yet again, in front of the gardeners, gamekeepers and staff alike, the Lady Clara Quinton and Mr. Grant once again showed a public display of affection and couldn't care less who viewed them doing so.

Certainly they did not.

Dear Reader,

Thank you for taking the time to read *To Fall For a Kiss*! I hope you enjoyed the fourth book in my Kiss the Wallflower series. Lady Clara and Stephen Grant were an enemies to lovers story that just begged to be written. They did spar together in A Midsummer Kiss, and I knew right then that these two had to fall in love.

I'm forever grateful to my readers, so if you're able, I would appreciate an honest review of *To Fall For a Kiss*. As they say, feed an author, leave a review! You can contact me at tamaragillauthor@gmail.com or sign up to my newsletter to keep up with my writing news.

If you'd like to learn about book five in my Kiss the Wallflower series, *A Duke's Wild Kiss*, please read on. I have included chapter one for your reading pleasure.

Tamara Gill

A DUKE'S WILD KISS

KISS THE WALLFLOWER, BOOK 5

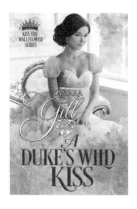

Miss Olivia Quinton is certain a marriage proposal is imminent, but her hopes are dashed when her gentleman admirer moves his attentions to another at a country house party. Disappointed by these turns of events and seeing the man for the fiend he is, Olivia hatches a plan of revenge. With the aid of Duke Hamlyn, she sets out to make her past love interest pay for his betrayal.

. . .

Jasper Abraham, Duke Hamlyn, did not think his Season would be taken up with helping a bedeviling chit in gaining her revenge. Everything would work out splendidly well if he hadn't already agreed to help his friend keep Olivia away from him during the house party and remaining Season.

Thrown together with opposite goals, Jasper cannot help but wonder why anyone would overthrow the delectable, sweet Olivia Quinton. Playing her fake beau is no chore, and the more time he spends with her, the more he wants to do a lot more than flirt with the chit.

Unfortunately, when games are played, there can be only one winner, but perhaps in this folly, everyone will lose.

CHAPTER 1

Kent 1810

"Will you do it for me, Hamlyn? We're not far from Chidding Hall, and I need your assurance you will support me with this matter. I need to have your promise, as my friend, that you will help me."

Jasper Abraham, Earl Hamlyn, gaped at his friend, Marquess Oglemoore. Had the fellow gone mad! He shook his head as the blood rushed back into his brain. "Absolutely not. Should I court Miss Quinton, she'd believe me to be enamored of her and possibly want a declaration of love and marriage soon after. If you led her to believe you liked her in town last Season and you did not, then you need to be the one who cleans up after your mistakes. I will not do it for you."

"You owe me, Hamlyn. Did I not step in at Bath just last month and stop those laborers from giving you a good thrashing? Which, by the way, I'm still unsure that you did not deserve."

"Now see here, how is it my fault that one of the men's sweethearts worked at the tavern and rented out her assets to those who could pay? I did not know she was betrothed."

"So you *did* sleep with her? I should have let them thrash you," Oglemoore said, raising his brow with a sarcastic tilt.

"I did no such thing. The woman seized my hand and placed it on her breast at the very moment her betrothed walked into the taproom. Had it been a bout of one-on-one, I would have had no qualms in thrashing the fool for allowing himself to be played so, but one on five and I drew the line." Jasper glared at his friend, disappointed. "What is more surprising to me is your seeking repayment of that service. I should have taken the bloodied nose and been done with it. I do not want to fool Miss Quinton in such a deceitful way. When she was in town last year, what I remember of her was a sweet, pleasant-looking woman. Are you sure you do not wish to court her instead of this Lady Athol Scott chit?"

"Absolutely certain. Miss Quinton is not for me. She's the niece of a duke, granddaughter of one, but other than the house she inherited from her father, and a notable portion, she has little else. Her cousin Lady Clara rules London society like the strict headmaster we had at Eton, and I'm not looking to be under her rule for the remainder of my days.

"I'm Marquess Oglemoore, my family has always married well. Lady Athol owns half of the Scottish lowlands. Imagine the hunting we can do if I marry her. No, Athol suits me very well."

"So, it's a love match, then?" Jasper said, his tone riddled with sarcasm.

Oglemoore's lips thinned into a disapproving line. "I do not love her, but I'm sure that will follow in time. I am fond of the chit, and so she will be my wife. But as for Miss Quinton, you must be the one to show more interest in her person. I need you to do this, truly. When she finds out that I'm courting someone else, she'll be right grieved. But if you, my handsome, English-titled friend show her there is more in the world than me, then she'll move on quick enough."

"And if she chooses me to be the man that she moves on with, what shall I do then? I do not want to be saddled with a wife. I have a mistress in town. A life." The horror of doing such a thing to an innocent woman did not sit well with Jasper, no matter who he had waiting for him back in London. He hated lies and deceit above most things, and this did not sit well with him. Oglemoore ought to know better. That he did not was no act of a gentleman.

"Please, my old friend. I'm begging you."

Jasper sighed, glaring across the carriage as it turned through the gates of Chidding Hall. "Very well, but this more than pays back my debt and then some. You owe me by quite a lot."

Oglemoore beamed, clapping his legs with his hands. "I knew I could count on you, my good friend. I shall gladly pay you back tenfold for this. Thank you."

Jasper wasn't so sure he would ever be repaid for acting the lovesick fool trying to turn a woman's eye toward him and off another. Even so, he would do it for his friend since he seemed so desperate. He could be Miss Quinton's friend, guide her away. There need not be anything romantic between them. If he followed that rule, all would be well and work out in the end.

"We're here," Oglemoore said, sliding toward the door.

Jasper picked up his top hat, slapping it onto his head. "Let the games begin," he said, throwing his friend a small grimace.

Let the games begin indeed.

. . .

*O*livia swallowed the bile that rose in her throat at hearing her closest friend declare that she hoped to marry Elliott Keating, Marquess Oglemoore.

"We were introduced at a ball in London. He's affable, and I enjoyed his company. I look forward to seeing him attend the house party," Athol said, a small smile playing about her lips.

The world spun around Olivia, and she clasped her stomach, taking a deep breath to try to stop her stomach contents from making an appearance.

"I had no idea you were even acquainted?" she stated, quite shocked by the fact. Lord Oglemoore was not only one of the most highly placed gentlemen in the *ton*, but he was also one of the most handsome. There was not a feminine heart in London that did not flutter in his presence.

Last Season Olivia had happened upon Lord Oglemoore as he'd stumbled out of the supper room after slipping on some barberry ices. She had awkwardly caught him, but instead of acting the assaulted debutante, she had laughed off the collision, and they had been friends ever since.

"Oh, it's all a bit of a shock to me too. We met at Almacks one Wednesday evening. He asked me to dance, and I agreed. I like him, and I do believe he likes me as well. Or," her friend said, biting her lip, "I hope he does, at least. The ladies speak highly of him, and he seems determined to find a wife. I merely hope he chooses me."

"Of course," Olivia said, her mind reeling. "As a gentleman, I'm sure he will not play you false. If he's shown an interest in you and you return favorably, this house party may end with a betrothal announcement." Olivia smiled at her friend, whom she loved most dearly, but the idea that the one gentleman whom she'd believed to have wanted to court her was instead seemingly interested in Athol was indeed a bitter pill to swallow. How had she been so wrong to read his character and interest so incorrectly?

Athol chuckled. "I do hope so. I seem to have pinned all my hopes on him, even though I have many gentlemen in town who stated they were awaiting my return. But I like Lord Oglemoore best of them all. He will do for me, I believe."

Olivia stared at Athol, unsure what she was hearing was true. Athol was going to marry a man simply because of what? "I'm sorry, my dear, but why marry him if you only think him your best choice? Why not take your time? This is only your second Season. Find a gentleman who puts your heart in his hand and never lets it go."

Her friend shrugged, plopping a grape in her mouth. They were seated out on the terrace that overlooked the grounds of her cousin's estate, the day warm without a breath of wind in the air.

"If you haven't noticed, we are getting rather long in the tooth, Olivia dear. We're both from respectable families and will do well together. I never cared overly much for a marriage to be based on love. You know I've always been practical with those types of things."

Olivia nodded, looking out over the gardens, bewildered at her friend's words. If she did not love Lord Oglemoore, then why could she not leave him be? Leave him for her?

The sound of a carriage approaching caught her attention, and Olivia glanced to where the road leading into the estate became visible through the trees. A black, highly polished carriage flittered through the foliage—more guests she assumed.

Athol shot to her feet, checking her gown and hair. "This will be Lord Oglemoore now. He said he'd arrive today. I'm so thankful that Lady Clara was willing to invite him and his friend to stay for the house party too."

Olivia did not move, not sure if her legs would support her. What a fun party they would all make with the man she had pinned all her hopes upon and her best friend who was trying as hard as she might to gain an understanding with him. She inwardly groaned, wanting to vanish to her rooms instead of meeting the guests as she should.

"Come, Olivia. Let us go out to the front and welcome them."

Olivia nodded, following without a word. Athol strode ahead, every now and then stopping to call for Olivia to quicken her pace. They made the estate front just as the carriage rocked to a halt, a billow of dust and all.

Her cousin Lady Clara and her husband, Mr. Grant, were already waiting on the home's steps, a warm smile on their lips as they prepared to greet their guests. Clara met Olivia's gaze. Puzzlement crossed her features before she joined her on the graveled drive.

"Are you well, Olivia dear? You look somewhat pale." She reached out, touching her forehead. "You do not feel warm, is there something else that is bothering you?"

Besides the fact that her best friend wanted to marry the man she coveted as her husband, no everything was perfectly well. "It is nothing, I assure you. Perhaps I have had too much sun today."

A footman opened the carriage door, and Lord Oglemoore jumped out, clasping Mr. Grant's—Stephen to those who knew him well—hands in welcome. He then turned to Athol, who stood waiting close by. Pleasure crossed his features, and Olivia felt the devastation of his attachment to her friend to her core. He liked her, to his credit. More than she'd thought, considering Athol merely liked the fellow, not actually loved him. Even so, Lord Oglemoore smiled lovingly at her friend, and Olivia did not miss the blush that stole across her friend's cheeks.

The carriage dipped a second time, and another gentleman appeared in the door. Olivia glanced at the man who jumped out of the equipage, dismissing him when Lord Oglemoore spoke.

"How wonderful to be back here again. It has been too long, Lady Clara, since you've opened the house," he said, smiling at her cousin before his gaze met hers.

He stepped toward her but did not drop Athol's hand that sat upon his arm. "Miss Quinton. You are a welcome sight, to be sure. I hope you're well?"

Somehow in all the despondency that pumped through her veins, she remembered her manners and smiled. "I am well, Lord Oglemoore. It is good to see you again too."

Oglemoore gestured to the gentleman behind him, and for the first time, Olivia took in the other house guest. He was taller than his lordship, athletic in build and surprisingly handsome.

She frowned, feeling as if she'd met him before, but unable to place where.

He smiled in welcome, a contemplative look in his eye when his gaze landed on her.

"This is my friend, His Grace, the Duke of Hamlyn."

Stephen held out his hand to His Grace, shaking it. "It has been too long, Hamlyn. I'm glad you're able to make the trip to Kent."

"Thank you for having me stay and congratulations on your marriage," the duke said, in a honeyed, deep tone.

Olivia watched as the duke kissed her cousin's cheeks. She turned for the doors, ready to go inside where she may be able to slip away for a moment or two to gather her wits. The house party loomed like a week of torture, and she wasn't so sure she wanted to be here anymore.

Her escape was blocked when Clara caught up to her,

leading her into the drawing room where an array of refreshments and a light lunch were prepared.

"Where do you think you're disappearing to, my dear? You have guests whom you must help me with."

Olivia sighed, letting Clara lead her into the room. "I need to speak to you when you are free. It is imperative."

Clara glanced at her, her brow furrowed. "Of course. I knew something was troubling you. We shall speak as soon as we can."

"Thank you." Olivia blinked away the sting of tears as she watched Athol and Lord Oglemoore seat themselves together on the settee by the window that overlooked the river. The duke hovered near the unlit hearth, speaking to Stephen.

"I'll come to your room before dinner this evening, and we'll have a chat," Clara said, patting her hand in comfort.

"Thank you." Olivia seated herself on a single leather-backed chair, willing the time to go by fast. A shadow passed over her and she glanced up, only to meet the amused gaze of the duke. She raised one brow, contesting his inspection of her with one of her own. "Is something amiss, Your Grace? You're scrutinizing me as if I have a blemish on my nose." Her question was, she supposed, rather rude, but she was no longer in the mood to be congenial. When one's hope of happiness was stripped, one was allowed to be curt.

"I do believe we've met, Miss Quinton. Last Season, in fact," he answered, his lips catching Olivia's attention for a moment before she tore her gaze away.

She shrugged, not willing to admit she knew him as well. A passing acquaintance and nothing more. He certainly never asked her to dance, she remembered that all too well. "It is possible that our paths crossed, Your Grace. I've met many people over the last few years in London." Pity he had not deemed her worthy of his interest, for he was known as a most sought-after catch.

He kneeled beside her chair, his hand resting on the arm. Olivia glanced at it. Really, did the man have to invade her space as well as ask her questions about a Season she'd prefer to forget?

"I assumed when you did not return to London this year that you had married." A light blush stole across his cheeks. Olivia narrowed her eyes, undecided if she would let him get away with what he was implying, that she was still unwed, an old maid in the making.

"I did not think gentlemen cared whether women they hardly favored to know married or not." He glanced at her, an amused look she found annoying filling his eyes. Did the man have no shame?

"I merely was surprised that an intelligent and beautiful woman such as yourself had not been swooped off her feet and carried into the sunset. That is all."

Olivia shut her mouth with a snap and tore her gaze away from him. He did not need to be so forward as that. Nor did she like his light flirtation with her. She did not want it from the duke.

She wanted it from Lord Oglemoore. Not that that was a possibility since the gentleman had his whole purpose fixed on her best friend. "I have not found anything to tempt me to the altar, my lord."

"Is that so?" he stated, glancing at his friend and then back to her. Olivia refused to blush or break her gaze. To do so would give credence to what he was saying, and she would not give him that pleasure. He continued to stare, not giving an inch on their little challenge and her blush deepened, their fixation on each other growing awkward.

Stephen cleared his throat, coming to stand beside Olivia.

"Everything well, my dear?" he asked her, touching her shoulder.

Olivia nodded, cursing that she had to look away before others noticed their frivolous game and made a comment.

"Of course. His Grace was just telling me how fond he is of your home and would like a tour," she lied.

Olivia stood and strode from the room before her cousin's husband asked if she would do the honors. Under no circumstance was she in the mood to play tour guide, and certainly not to a man who seemed amused by what was going on between her and Lord Oglemoore.

She strode toward the stairs, not caring she did not resemble the duke's granddaughter she was. She needed to reach the sanctity of her room. A place she could think and plan.

What that plan was, however, she was not certain just yet. Would she try to dissuade Athol into marrying Lord Oglemoore should he ask? Over the years, she'd certainly heard plenty of tales about the gentleman's antics both in London and Bath.

Some of which had made even herself blush a time or two, but after his kindness toward her last Season she had dismissed the stories as false.

Olivia made her room, closing and locking the door before she flopped onto the bed. How could this have happened? She had been so sure of his regard for her. Last Season, Lord Oglemoore sought her out, danced and took supper with her. The horrible thought crossed her mind that it was all for show, a game he enjoyed to play with unattached women.

She sighed, staring up at the wooden beams lining her bedroom ceiling. There were two choices she could make regarding this awful turn of events. She could wish them well and move on with her life. Have another Season and see if any offers were forthcoming.

To parade herself again would be a humiliation she doubted she could ever recover from, and she wasn't certain she had it in her to do again. To walk into a ballroom, night after night, and try to find love.

She swiped a tear from her cheek, annoyance thrumming through her. Athol deserved better than a man who would treat her friend or any woman with so little respect. What was stopping him from throwing Athol aside when someone better in his opinion came along? Nothing.

Olivia sat up, thinking of what could be done. He would pay for his callousness. She would show Athol he was unworthy of her during the week that he was here. Olivia chewed her bottom lip, frowning in thought. But how, that was the question, and one she would mull over before tomorrow.

Want to read more? Get A Duke's Wild Kiss today!

LORDS OF LONDON SERIES
AVAILABLE NOW!

Dive into these charming historical romances! In this six-book series by Tamara Gill, Darcy seduces a virginal duke, Cecilia's world collides with a roguish marquess, Katherine strikes a deal with an unlucky earl and Lizzy sets out to conquer a very wicked Viscount. These stories plus more adventures in the Lords of London series!

LEAGUE OF UNWEDDABLE GENTLEMEN SERIES AVAILABLE NOW!

Fall into my latest series, where the heroines have to fight for what they want, both regarding their life and love. And where the heroes may be unweddable to begin with, that is until they meet the women who'll change their fate. The League of Unweddable Gentlemen series is available now!

TO VEX A VISCOUNT

TO DARE A DUCHESS

TO MARRY A MARCHIONESS

LORDS OF LONDON - BOOKS 1-3 BUNDLE

LORDS OF LONDON - BOOKS 4-6 BUNDLE

To Marry a Rogue Series

ONLY AN EARL WILL DO

ONLY A DUKE WILL DO

ONLY A VISCOUNT WILL DO

ONLY A MARQUESS WILL DO

ONLY A LADY WILL DO

A Time Traveler's Highland Love Series

TO CONQUER A SCOT

TO SAVE A SAVAGE SCOT

TO WIN A HIGHLAND SCOT

Time Travel Romance

DEFIANT SURRENDER

A STOLEN SEASON

Scandalous London Series

A GENTLEMAN'S PROMISE

A CAPTAIN'S ORDER

A MARRIAGE MADE IN MAYFAIR

SCANDALOUS LONDON - BOOKS 1-3 BUNDLE

High Seas & High Stakes Series

HIS LADY SMUGGLER

HER GENTLEMAN PIRATE

HIGH SEAS & HIGH STAKES - BOOKS 1-2 BUNDLE

Daughters Of The Gods Series
BANISHED-GUARDIAN-FALLEN
DAUGHTERS OF THE GODS - BOOKS 1-3 BUNDLE

Stand Alone Books
TO SIN WITH SCANDAL
OUTLAWS

ABOUT THE AUTHOR

Tamara is an Australian author who grew up in an old mining town in country South Australia, where her love of history was founded. So much so, she made her darling husband travel to the UK for their honeymoon, where she dragged him from one historical monument and castle to another.

A mother of three, her two little gentlemen in the making, a future lady (she hopes) and a part-time job keep her busy in the real world, but whenever she gets a moment's peace she loves to write romance novels in an array of genres, including regency, medieval and time travel.

www.tamaragill.com
tamaragillauthor@gmail.com